# *A Candlelight Ecstasy Romance*™

## HE WAS HYPNOTIZING HER WITH THAT HUSKY, DEEP VOICE. . . .

Lacey couldn't find the strength of will to extricate herself. Her body was luxuriating in the random patterns he was outlining on her flesh, finding a compelling, enchanting quality in his pantherlike body, in the heat of him. Her mind longed to sink beneath the spell his voice created in the darkness— to sink down onto the magic carpet and be carried away. Her lashes fluttered, then lay still against her cheeks as she awaited the next caress. . . .

# SPELLBOUND

*Jayne Castle*

## A CANDLELIGHT ECSTASY ROMANCE™

Published by
Dell Publishing Co., Inc.
1 Dag Hammarskjold Plaza
New York, New York 10017

Dell ® TM 681510, Dell Publishing Co., Inc.

Candlelight Ecstasy Romance™ is a trademark of
Dell Publishing Co., Inc., New York, New York.

ISBN 0-440-18034-1

Printed in the United States of America
First printing—November 1982

To Our Readers:

We have been delighted with your enthusiastic response to Candlelight Ecstasy Romances™ and we thank you for the interest you have shown in this exciting series.

In the upcoming months, we will continue to present the distinctive, sensuous love stories you have come to expect only from Ecstasy. We look forward to bringing you many more books from your favorite authors and also, the very finest work from new authors of contemporary romantic fiction.

As always, we are striving to present the unique, absorbing love stories that you enjoy most—books that are more than ordinary romance.

Your suggestions and comments are always welcome. Please write to us at the address below.

Sincerely,

The Editors
Candlelight Romances
1 Dag Hammarskjold Plaza
New York, N.Y. 10017

# CHAPTER ONE

"You were supposed to be much taller!"

Under normal circumstances Lacey Holbrook would have been horrified to hear herself blurting out such a thing to a stranger on her doorstep. But she was feeling far too anxious at the moment to worry about the niceties. Face it, she thought disgustedly, she was feeling more than anxious. Her inner thoughts had strayed more than once over the border of anxiety into the foreign territory of fear. And fear was no observer of the proprieties.

Besides, she added in immediate, if silent, self-justification, the accusation about his height was only a minor charge compared to all the others she could have made. He was not what she had ordered at all!

"I know the height isn't exactly as specified," the stranger drawled in a deep, laconic voice that unexpectedly reminded Lacey of a panther's growl, and even more unexpectedly touched a tiny chord of memory. "But we're out of the six-foot-three-inch bodybuilder variety this season. Perhaps if you'd gotten your specifications in before last Christmas we could have—"

"Oh, for heaven's sake! Come in," Lacey interrupted ungraciously, stepping aside. Six foot one inch would have been nice, she told herself, let alone six foot three inches. With her own five feet eight inches she had wanted at least a six-foot male just for a proper sense of scale. What she had gotten, judging from the eye-to-eye contact, was closer to five feet nine inches, perhaps a tad over. And she hated beards!

"Thank you," the man murmured, glancing around with undisguised wariness as he moved into the black-granite tiled foyer. "I think."

He peered cautiously ahead, following the path of the black granite as it flowed into a living room done in starkly modern black, chrome, and white.

Lacey ignored his reaction to the decor. She was accustomed to such reactions, had designed the apartment with the sole purpose of achieving them, in fact. Impact was everything in her business.

And speaking of impact, what was it about this stranger that was disturbing a memory far back in her mind, having a slight disorienting impact on her sense of awareness? Impatiently she brushed aside the feeling. She had far more important matters to worry about.

He followed as she led the way into the living room with its white walls and ceiling and black floor. Silently she motioned to him to take one of the black and chrome chaise longues and settled herself restlessly on the black leather banquette near the window. Stacks of black leather pillows formed a backdrop for the scarlet and peacock-blue silk jumpsuit she was wearing.

"Look," her visitor began a little drily as his eyes went to the huge black steel sculpture on the white wall across from him, "I don't mind paying a debt, but if I'm being invited to fulfill the role of sacrifice at the weekly meeting of your witches' coven, I think you should know I'm not really the martyr type."

Lacey raised a deliberately skeptical brow. "You mean to say Wesley Merlin would rather give me the thirty thousand plus interest than a prize specimen such as yourself?"

Tawny brown eyes, framed by a wealth of gold-shot, light brown hair and a full beard and mustache locked with her own hazel gaze across the width of the room. Quite suddenly it wasn't just his voice that reminded Lacey of a panther and quickened some vague chord of recognition. There was something about him—the lean, rangy way he moved, those eyes, that voice. Where could she possibly have met him?

"My father is dead, Lacey," he told her coldly. "He was killed two years ago in a sailing accident."

"Your father!" Lacey gasped, taken aback. Everything clicked into place, including the hints of recognition. This was Jed Merlin. She hadn't seen him since she was thirteen years old . . . and had made such a fool of herself! Even as the embarrassing memory came back, she willed away the small flush. Thirteen-year-old girls were always making fools of themselves by having crushes on older men. It went with the territory. And Jed, as she recalled wryly, had been most understanding.

"In your conversation with my lawyer, you stated you wanted the services of a presentable male in lieu of payment on the debt my father owed yours. I'm afraid I was the only one immediately available. Take me or leave me," he said with a mildness which belied the faint hint of warning in his eyes. Lacey frowned slightly as more memories returned. The young man she had known had always been rather indulgent with her, but even at thirteen she had known something of the rocklike willpower laying close to the surface.

*Funny,* came an errant thought, *I would have thought Jed Merlin would have turned out differently. I would have guessed he'd have matured into a powerful, dynamic man, not an aging hippie.*

She bit her lip. "I'm . . . I'm sorry, Jed. I didn't know about your father's death." The news was something of a shock. It could change everything. But even more of a shock was Jed Merlin himself. She shook her head ruefully. "I didn't even recognize you."

"It's been a long time." His tawny gaze moved over her appraisingly. "The feeling is mutual. If I hadn't known who you were, I doubt that I'd have been able to recognize you. The last time I saw you was when you were thirteen and I was twenty." The mouth behind the full beard crooked in a teasing smile she remembered with unexpected clarity. "You were bent on maneuvering me even then, as I recall. I gather things haven't changed."

"Except that you were a little kinder then. You didn't accuse me of maneuvering you the day I proposed; you just told me I wasn't quite your type," Lacey shot back wryly. Sooner or later he was bound to bring up that embarrassing incident of her childhood. Better to get it over by reminding him herself! But in spite of all the self-possession her twenty-nine years had brought her, she couldn't quite meet his eyes for a moment.

"If it's any consolation, I've never forgotten your charming little business proposition," Jed chuckled. "It's the only time a woman has asked me to marry her in such a forthright, demanding way."

"Been dealing with more subtle types ever since, hmmm?"

"You were anything but subtle, as I recall," he grinned. "How was it you put it? Something about the two of us inheriting our fathers' business empires and uniting them through marriage? Then you looked me right in the eye and told me very matter-of-factly I was the perfect man for you."

Lacey winced in pained memory. It was all too true. She'd had a crush on Jed Merlin that wouldn't quit! "You'll have to forgive me," she murmured with acid sweetness. "From the perspective of my thirteen years of age, you looked a lot taller!"

The grin behind the beard moved into outright laughter. "Grew up to like them tall, dark, and handsome, huh?"

"You appear not to have done much growing up at all," she shot back easily. "What happened? Did your evolutionary development get stuck somewhere in the sixties?"

He shrugged, shoulders moving under the scrungy, patchwork denim jacket he wore with a smoothness that suggested an easy masculine strength. "Too bad our families lost track of each other over the years. It would have been interesting to follow your development too. You seemed to have kept up with the times, Lacey, love."

"Don't call me that," she muttered, annoyed at the endearment. It was one of the slender threads upon which she'd constructed her childhood fantasy of marrying Jed Merlin. He, of course, had only used the term with the greatest of offhand casualness. Looking back at the few occasions when she'd been taken for a visit to the Merlin estate in northern California, Lacey knew Jed had never treated her with anything other than brotherly affection.

"Sorry," he apologized unrepentantly. "But the comment appears to be accurate. You fulfilled your promise as a youngster, from the looks of things. Your father was going to turn the handling of his affairs over to you eventually, as I recall, and you were more than happy to be groomed for the position."

"Unlike yourself," she reminded him with a neutralness that belied the disapproval in her eyes. "I can still recall the battles you had with your father over the subject of your future. I take it you managed to resist conforming. Have you been living the life of an upper-class dropout all these years?" Just what she needed, Lacey thought disgustedly, a thirty-six-year-old free spirit who had never grown up! "I'd have thought you'd have matured by now."

"You're looking at Jed Merlin, scion of the family, heir to the fortune, and the one in charge of paying off family debts. At your service," he mocked.

Lacey lifted reproachful eyes toward heaven as she tried to analyze the change in the situation. This wasn't going at all as she had planned and there really wasn't time to devise a new scheme. Rick Clayton would be back in town in a few days and she wanted everything in place by then. Too much depended on it.

"You needn't look so disappointed," Jed went on calmly. "You didn't exactly grow up to be my type either."

Lacey shook her head automatically, eyeing his figure as he sprawled with catlike ease on the black and chrome lounge chair. With an almost unconsciously assessing glance that had become second nature in her work, she surveyed the man. It was impossible to see what he looked like behind that beard, but the tawny eyes and the flash of even white teeth were quite visible. Neither feature, she realized in vague surprise, held any sign of the weakness that should have been evident, given his years of lotus-eating. The knowledge gave her a momentary pause. Lacey had long since learned to trust her design instincts. But there was really no time to dwell on the matter now.

He was wearing, in addition to the faded denim jacket, a pair of equally faded and worn jeans. She caught sight of a plaid shirt of uncertain color underneath the unfastened jacket. Scuffed leather boots and a silver belt buckle of the hand-crafted variety completed the outfit.

He was quite right, she decided ruefully, she probably hadn't grown into anything resembling the sort of woman he undoubtedly preferred.

"For one thing," Jed was saying with more than a touch of maliciousness, as if he'd overheard her thoughts, "I like my women small and fragile." The tawny eyes raked the outline of her less-than-fragile figure, lingering pointedly on the fullness of hips that were a little too rounded for the sleek Los Angeles look Lacey wanted.

She shifted resentfully on the black cushions as the golden brown eyes moved lazily upward, taking in the softness of her high, rounded breasts and the contour of a waist which, while in proportion to the rest of her figure, was hardly the size that could be spanned by a man's hands!

No, she wasn't the fragile type, Lacey thought, reassuring herself in the next breath that neither was she in the least fat. On low self-esteem days she sometimes thought of herself as plump, but on high self-esteem days she de-

13

cided she was well proportioned. In between she told herself that it was good to capitalize on her five-foot-eight-inch figure by having a body that had a certain presence. As an interior designer in Los Angeles, one needed presence!

But she was sure her lack of fragility wasn't the only factor that Jed Merlin wouldn't find attractive. He probably saw her short, deceptively casual nut-brown hair as too sophisticated for his taste. He undoubtedly preferred the long flowing tresses of a more earthy sort of female. And Lacey knew from having glanced periodically in the mirror over the past twenty-nine years that she lacked a delicate, fragile face too.

She was enough of a designer to know the wide hazel eyes, firm chin, and straight nose comprised a face that radiated a certain intelligent energy, but she wasn't at all convinced Jed Merlin would appreciate such an attraction. She was no gentle leftover flower child. Lacey Holbrook was strong, dynamic, businesslike, and blessed with a slightly arrogant style. Today that hint of arrogance was augmented by an edge of concealed anxiety.

Lifting one silk-clad shoulder in casual unconcern, she smiled acidly at her visitor. "So I could probably win three falls out of five in a wrestling match with you. Don't worry about it. I didn't ask you here to wrestle."

The tawny eyes narrowed coolly. "Thanks for the reassurance. I might point out, however, that what counts in a wrestling match between a man and a woman is not how many times the lady wins, but which of them takes the last fall."

Lacey stilled, catching her breath at the essence of unsubtly assured masculinity that seemed to come at her in

14

a wave. Then she moved in a small, restless fashion, telling herself fiercely it was sheer temper that was bringing the flush of red up to burn her cheekbones. She was not going to admit this—this—hippie had the power to elicit so much as a twinge of feminine wariness in her!

"Mr. Merlin," she began pointedly.

"Please don't call me that," he interrupted. "It makes me sound like a reincarnation of King Arthur's sorcerer!"

A flash of humor drove out some of Lacey's temper. "And you don't see yourself as a wizard?"

"Hardly," he grimaced. "Although it might be useful if you really are into witchcraft." Once again he examined the starkly modern room.

"The apartment isn't decorated as a modern witch's habitat," she grumbled, following his gaze. "If you were more acquainted with current trends in interior design, you would recognize the essential simplicity and sensuousness of the minimalist style. Everything here"—she waved a hand dramatically at her surroundings—"is both elegant and functional, composed of rich materials and textures. A perfect background for the dramatic color and life people bring with them into the room."

"You're not a practicing witch?" he demanded skeptically.

"Don't be ridiculous."

"One never knows about you Los Angeles types," he demurred. "Well, it's a relief to know you're not going to use me in some bizarre ritual," he went on with a new crispness as his gaze swung back to her austerely composed features. "Now, suppose you tell me exactly what it is you do want from the Merlins, Lacey."

"If your lawyer related my wishes . . ." She started only

15

to have him hold up a warding-off hand. It was a nice hand, she thought in surprise. Strong and tanned. The shape of the fingers reminded her of the sensitivity locked in his touch. A sensitivity she had witnessed the day she had watched him soothe and tend one of the estate dogs that had been struck by a car. The dog had quieted immediately beneath the touch of those fingers. Damn! Her imagination was really working overtime today, dredging up memories she could well do without.

"I know," he growled. "You asked for someone tall and, I believe, the word was *presentable*. Unfortunately you're stuck with me. What the hell led you to remember that old debt in the first place?"

"To tell you the truth, I probably wouldn't have found out about it if I hadn't had to go through my father's papers after he was killed a few years ago."

"I see," he murmured, deep voice softening slightly. "I hadn't realized you'd lost your father too."

She inclined her head in quiet acceptance of the formal condolence. "As I said, the debt seems to have been a private arrangement between my father and yours. I have no interest in calling in the money."

"Generous of you," he remarked grimly.

"But," she continued deliberately, "I find myself in a somewhat awkward situation. I need a little help and, quite frankly, I wanted to use someone who was not among my circle of friends."

"The operative word being *use* I suppose?"

In spite of the seriousness of her situation, Lacey's mouth quirked with barely repressed laughter. "Such cynicism, Jed Merlin. But I imagine it's because there's a slight generation gap between us. Do I make you ner-

16

vous?" she purred. "The older generation often is in the presence of the younger one."

White teeth flashed for an instant behind the beard, and Lacey thought she detected a measure of purely masculine appreciation for her sharp tongue.

"I have no objection these days to younger women, Lacey. And no problem relating to them. It's those of you turning thirty and getting desperate who make me nervous."

"Don't worry," she shot back. "I wouldn't dream of trying to force reality and responsibility on you at your age! Besides, one of the things I've tried since we last saw each other is marriage. It was a disaster," she confided stonily. "It verified, in fact, all the lessons you tried to teach me that miserable day I asked you to marry me when I grew up."

He looked at her with curiosity. "As I recall, my parents had just gotten a divorce and I was a little bitter."

"You made it quite clear you never intended to marry— me or anyone else. I suppose you were moving into your free-spirited stage even then. A stage you don't appear to have outgrown. You said the odds were against two people being able to spend a lifetime together and you were interested only in a series of affairs." Lacey smiled a little grimly. "In that one respect we appear to have shared a parallel development, although I didn't come to the same conclusion until a couple of years ago when my marriage broke up."

"What happened, Lacey?" he asked almost gently. She thought she caught a flicker of some of the old big-brother indulgence he'd once favored her with. It annoyed her.

17

The thought of Jed Merlin playing big brother had never been pleasant but now it rankled worse than ever.

"Statistics happened," she told him with a false brightness. "You know as well as I do that here in California the divorce rate runs over fifty percent and is still climbing. Lord only knows what made me think I could beat the odds. A last holdover of optimism from my childhood, I suppose. But having my husband fall in love with another woman completed my education."

"You no longer see me as the perfect marriage candidate then?" he asked interestedly.

"Hardly. Would you mind if this conversation got back to the main subject?"

"Not at all. You don't want me as a sacrifice, either in the black arts or in matrimony. And you say you don't want the thirty thousand my father owed your father. Which leaves . . . ?"

"Which leaves me in the position of asking a personal favor in repayment of that debt," Lacey finished, drawing a deep breath.

"I'm listening," he sighed, stretching his jean-clad legs out in front of him. The heels of the boots slid on the polished granite floor with a small squeak and the denim material was pulled tautly across smoothly muscled thighs. Lacey found herself having to look away. What was the matter with her? She had a complicated situation on her hands and she certainly had no business being distracted by a character like this! Jed Merlin had not grown up to be the man of her dreams!

"This is a little difficult to explain, Jed."

"That's all right. I have a surprising amount of native intelligence," he assured her drily. "Not a huge amount, you understand, but more than you might expect from someone as simple and down-to-earth–looking as myself."

"What I require from you shouldn't strain your faculties! However," she went on, surveying him with a deliberately critical eye, "it may put a certain amount of stress on your sense of identity and your no-doubt well-developed spirit of breezy independence."

"I get it. It has something to do with me not being tall, dark, and handsome, right?"

"You're very perceptive."

"You're going to try and make me over in the proper image?" he guessed ruefully, glancing down at his faded denims.

"If you're agreeable," she nodded briskly.

"What can I say? I owe you thirty thousand dollars," he shrugged.

"You don't owe it." Lacey frowned at him. The news of his father's death was unsettling. She really had no hold on the son.

"I fully intend to honor my father's debts."

The flash of arrogant pride in the narrowed, tawny eyes caused Lacey to blink uncertainly. She suppressed the uneasy reaction. Nevertheless, she was forcibly reminded of the fact that at twenty Jed Merlin had not only had a deep, masculine pride; that same pride and natural will-power had made him very difficult to manipulate. She had not only failed at it on several occasions using the wiles of a thirteen-year-old; his own father had failed at it and the elder Merlin had had all the power and authority of the Merlin empire to bring into action against his son. Jed had often been kind, even indulgent, but she didn't remember him ever being the sort of man one could maneuver. Ah, well, he *must* be a different type of man now. Lacey just wished she didn't keep getting those twinges of fantasy in which he reminded her of a lazy, potentially dangerous panther!

"Thank you," she murmured. "This won't take long. I'm only asking for an evening of your time, perhaps two evenings. That should be enough."

"Enough for what?" he asked suspiciously.

Lacey's mouth curved downward in a cold smile. "Enough to gain me a very small but very important diamond."

A sunstreaked brow arched upward in silent inquiry. The suddenly familiar mannerism brought another flood of memories. Among them was the reminder that Jed Merlin had always been a very intelligent man. Regardless of what he'd done with his life, there was no reason to think he wasn't still annoyingly perceptive. She was going to have to make this good.

"No, I'm not asking you to do any breaking and entering," she said lightly.

"You're hoping to acquire this small, important diamond from a man, then? I'm to be used to make some rich fool jealous?" he demanded stonily.

"In a way . . ."

"Of all the idiotic, stupid, crazy female ideas! Talk about not growing up!"

Lacey sat up with sudden, intent fierceness, her eyes full of her anger. Damn it! She was no longer thirteen! She was the one in charge here! "You have no notion of what's involved!"

"I can make a damn good guess. Some man whose potential is more than thirty thousand is involved!"

"Given the fact that we both know your inheritance was hardly a trifling sum, you're in no position to ridicule someone else who has money. Just because you choose to dress and act as if you're one of those who has no use for it, don't try telling me you don't find it convenient on occasion to draw on the Merlin fortune!"

"What do you know of the Merlin fortune?" There was a speculative coolness in him as he asked the question and Lacey decided he'd never gotten over the resentment he'd felt when Wesley Merlin had tried to force him into the family business. It was true she'd been only thirteen years old the last time she'd seen Jed, but she'd been alert to every nuance in him, watching him with the eyes of a young girl with a crush.

Jed and his father had fought continuously, even in front of Lacey and her parents. Jed had resisted Wesley's coercing ways with all the passion of a young man who sees his whole life waiting for him and doesn't want to waste it running a business in which he has no interest.

Jed would never know it, Lacey thought ruefully, but one of the reasons she'd couched her proposal in business terms was that she had thought it would stand a better chance of being accepted. In a painfully juvenile fashion she'd attempted to make him more amenable to his fate by showing him she shared the same one. It had never occurred to Lacey that Jed would continue resisting his father to the bitter end. But he had.

"I remember the estate," she pointed out. "And my father often mentioned your father's success."

"Most of which was acquired several years after your dad made that loan to mine, I believe," Jed remarked.

"Your father was a self-made man. You should be proud of him!"

"I'd have been prouder if he'd remembered to pay back some of his debts! Like that thirty grand, for instance!"

"My father chose not to press for it. I'm sure if he had, Wesley would have repaid it at once. It probably was forgotten over the years."

"You needn't defend both of our parents," he sighed. "What's past is past. You, unlike your father, have chosen to call in the tab. I, in my parent's absence, will attempt to make good on it. Hopefully, you will have your diamond ring in a reasonably short period of time and I can be on my way."

"Back to your lotus-eating life-style? How do you manage things, Jed? Let that lawyer run everything while you just sit back on some communal farm and read philosophy?"

"Lucky you didn't succeed in getting me to marry you, isn't it?" he retorted smoothly. "Think how you would have worn yourself out nagging me all these years!"

"I certainly wouldn't have let you ruin your potential!" Good Lord! What was the matter with her? What did she care about Jed's potential now? She had her own problems!

"Perhaps it would have gone the other way," he suggested. "I might have been able to keep you from turning into a cool, hard-edged, flashy southern California businesswoman. How does it feel, Lacey, living your life with an eye out for the main chance? Being on the cutting edge?"

"Gratifying. Now, if you don't mind . . ."

"Ah, yes. Tell me what it is you want, Lacey, and let's get it over with."

Lacey gnawed thoughtfully on her lower lip, the fingers of her left hand drumming on the leather of the banquette cushion. "It's not quite that simple."

"So tell me how unsimple it's going to be," he groaned.

Lacey hesitated. Now that the crucial moments of the hastily concocted plan were upon her, the nervousness was increasing by leaps and bounds. She fought it, getting a firm grip on her imagination and an even firmer hold on her outward expression. Cool and hard-edged, was she? Nothing like living up to the image!

She was fairly certain her efforts at inner self-control were not going to endear her to Jed Merlin. He would see the coolness in her eyes and hauteur edging her lips and put it down to a sophisticated hardness. He would have no way of knowing the strain that expression was shielding.

But everything had gone relatively smoothly so far, hadn't it? Smoothly, if she overlooked the unexpected shock of finding Jed Merlin on her doorstep.

Even that could be dealt with, she decided bravely, the artist in her assessing the lean, coordinated body under the denims. He moved well and even seated there was an underlying feeling of restrained power in him. For some reason that sense of strength was oddly comforting to her.

It remained to be seen what lay under the beard, but her recollection of his face suggested the basic features would be acceptable. Jed hadn't been handsome, but there had been a rough, masculine attraction. And in the right clothes he would look good, she decided. Very good. That catlike grace in him would set its own style.

She shouldn't have to worry too much about his manners or his ability to handle himself in social situations either. She'd be willing to bet that a successful man like Wesley Merlin would have seen to it that his son and heir apparent had been properly raised and educated. Yes, the raw material was there and she was a designer, wasn't she?

"It's not just the small diamond I'm after," Lacey plunged in cautiously.

One light brown brow climbed again, but Jed said nothing. He had the air of a man awaiting the inevitable. A sort of grim resignation that touched a chord of humor in Lacey.

"I also want an invitation to stay at your family estate for a couple of weeks. Perhaps as long as a month," she amended honestly.

A heavy silence descended. Lacey waited, striving for a certain nonchalance she was far from feeling. Internally she was madly rounding up butterflies. What was she going to do if he refused?

"Two weeks to a month on the Merlin estate?" Jed repeated her request as if he wanted to be very sure he'd gotten it right. He eyed her askance.

"Well?" she prompted with more eagerness than she might have wished. "Is that too much to ask?"

It was his turn to hesitate, and Lacey could have sworn a spark of dry amusement lit the gold of his eyes for just an instant before he said quite silkily, "No. Even at the most exorbitant estimates it's hard to see how two weeks at my home could add up to a thirty-thousand-dollar vacation package!"

"Two weeks to a month," she reminded him, smiling in her relief. He was going to agree to it! Visions of snarling guard dogs, high walls, and grim security personnel danced happily in her head. "Plus the one or two nights work I shall be requiring beforehand."

"You're sure this is all you want in exchange for a thirty-thousand-dollar debt?"

"I'm sure." Heaven knew she felt guilty enough asking him to pay off a debt owed to her father. That business had been strictly between their parents and if she hadn't been in such a difficult situation she would never have pursued the obligation.

"Then," he muttered, shoving his hands into the front pockets of his jeans and regarding her under a straight line of bunched brows, "I suppose you'd better explain exactly what the one or two nights work is going to entail."

Lacey took a breath and leaned forward intently, the intelligent energy in her face erasing some of the too-casual sophistication. "It won't be all that hard on you unless you're unduly attached to that beard!"

He raised one hand to stroke the offending feature, tawny eyes turning deeply meditative. "I thought women liked beards." Was he laughing at her?

"Not unless they're well trimmed!"

"I'm crushed. Well, it's cheaper to grow it back than come up with thirty thousand in cash," he decided philosophically. "I've only got one serious question before I agree."

Lacey looked at him inquiringly.

"Is this other guy a lot bigger than I am?" he calmly inquired. No, he was not afraid, Lacey could see, simply curious. Oh, yes, Jed Merlin exuded a sense of latent power—power that would make him a formidable match for any opponent, Lacey was sure.

"Don't worry! I'm not going to involve you in a fight!" Lacey snapped.

Jed revealed his disbelief. "You're out to make some poor sucker jealous enough to propose, aren't you? Isn't that what this is all about? I'm to be used to force his hand?"

Lacey shook her head emphatically, the nut-brown curls moving in an intriguing disarray exactly as planned by her expensive Beverly Hills hairdresser. "You've got it all wrong!"

"What about that diamond you mentioned?" he retorted stonily.

"Oh, I'm after the diamond, all right," Lacey confirmed readily enough, her mouth quirking upward as she saw his disdainful confusion. "But this diamond will be set on a small pendant, not a ring. It's Rick Clayton's standard farewell gift to his girl friends. Rick has a lot of class," she added, the quirking mouth lifting into a brief, laughing grin.

"You're joking! You want *out* of a relationship?" Jed looked at her a little blankly.

"Exactly."

"Have you tried just telling him politely that it's over?" he suggested wryly.

This was where things got a little shaky, Lacey reminded herself. "It wouldn't work in this case." She saw no need to go into details. The less Jed Merlin knew, the better.

"The guy's so besotted over you he wouldn't let you go?"

Lacey's hazel gaze narrowed at the sarcasm. "I may not look like your dream of the earth-mother–bread-baking type, but, believe it or not, *some* men do find me mildly interesting."

A slow, sardonic smile appeared through the beard, and the gold eyes gleamed with a masculine appraisal that knew no life-style boundaries. "I wouldn't dream of implying you aren't interesting, Lacey Holbrook. If the truth be known, I'm beginning to find you somewhat fascinating. Not terribly bright, perhaps, but fascinating."

"What do you mean, not very bright?" Her chin rose aggressively.

"Any woman who thinks some man is going to give her a diamond pendant when he finds out she's been playing around with another man has got to be lacking in the brains department!"

"I've told you! It's Rick's way of letting a woman know she's out of his life. He's got a reputation for it, and he likes that. He thinks it gives him style."

"What if he decides to make an exception in this case?" Jed challenged coolly. "What if he decides he'd rather have you than a little style?"

"He won't," Lacey said with great assurance. "He's not in love with me. I'm not sure Rick is capable of loving anyone," she added reflectively.

"There's a little matter of male pride to be taken into consideration!"

"I agree. I'm counting on that factor, believe me. Rick

27

will want to be the one to break things off, and I'm going to provide the excuse!"

"Me." Jed's disgust was growing rapidly, Lacey realized. Well, his was not to reason why.

"You."

"I gather you're going through this charade in order to get the diamond? If you were the one to break things off, there would be no farewell rock forthcoming?" he asked scornfully.

Lacey caught her breath. The easiest thing all around was to have Jed believe exactly that. "Something like that," she smiled politely.

"Tell me," he charged unexpectedly, "why don't you just demand the thirty thousand from me? Surely that amounts to more than the diamond pendant will be worth? You could kiss the pendant good-bye and collect the Merlin debt instead!"

"I don't want your money!" Lacey reacted instantly to the accusation.

"Lacey, this doesn't make any sense," he snapped abruptly, an underlying edge of steel in his voice that took her by surprise. For the first time she began to wonder whether Jed Merlin had done something else in life besides rebel against his upper-class background. Where would a man who had lived a careless, undirected existence gain that particular hint of honed strength?

"I don't care if it makes any sense to you or not," she told him crisply. "The truth of the matter is that I don't have any right to the thirty thousand your father owed mine and we both know it. What I'm really asking of you is a favor based on that old debt."

He considered that for a long moment. "I see. You

don't think you could actually force me to fork over the money, is that it?"

"Of course not. If I pressed for the money you could probably find a way to keep from having to pay me. I'm aware of that. What I'm counting on is that you won't mind doing me this favor instead. In return I'll guarantee to forget the debt and you'll know there will never be any need to fight me in court."

"A court fight you couldn't afford," he said with a pouncing sound in his voice. Light had obviously dawned. "I get it. You know it would be expensive trying to force payment on the debt through legal channels so you're willing to settle out of court, as it were, by asking this favor instead."

Lacey lifted one shoulder in an elaborately unconcerned shrug. And he had the nerve to imply she wasn't very intelligent! Little did he know how easily he'd just been manipulated! Lacey didn't need thirty thousand dollars that weren't really hers to claim anyway. What she needed was a place to hide. And she needed it without a lot of involved explanations.

"Okay, that makes a little more sense," Jed was saying slowly. "So let's get on with the grand scheme. What is it, exactly, that you want me to do?"

Lacey hesitated, telling herself over and over that she had, indeed, just manipulated him very easily. So why did her feminine instincts still insist on trying to get a warning of some sort through to her brain? Was it because they remembered that the Jed of twenty had not been so easily handled? Or were they reacting strictly to the subtle warning buried in those catlike eyes? *What am I getting into?*

She brushed the thought aside. There were really very

few options open to her. She would have to work with what she had.

"Isn't it obvious?" she murmured with a flippancy she didn't feel. "I want you to compromise me. Subtly, you understand, but . . . sufficiently."

30

# CHAPTER TWO

"Do you have to sit out here like an anxious mother waiting for her son to have his first haircut?" Jed Merlin rasped under his breath an hour later as Lacey sank into a chair in the waiting area of an expensive men's styling salon.

She reached for a magazine on men's fashions and shot him a repressive glance. "Be grateful I'm not going to stand over the stylist's shoulder and supervise! I have a lot at stake here."

"You think you have a lot at stake! This represents eighteen months of hard work," he protested, indicating the gold-shot beard.

"Or lack thereof," she retorted sweetly. "Now remember what I said to tell Armand. I want something very current—casual, but classy. He'll know what I mean."

Jed muttered something inaudible but emphatic and turned on one booted heel to announce his presence to the receptionist. Lacey smiled to herself as she watched him disappear without a backward glance into the gleaming, ultra-modern interior of the salon. He was like a panther let loose at a garden party. A little wild-looking, untamed, and definitely out of place.

She considered her own mental description. Likening him to a panther in civilized surroundings didn't seem right. With his careless, go-to-hell clothes, the full beard, and the general air of disgust toward his expensive surroundings, she should have visualized him as a petulant, overage hippie. But as she watched him stride away, it was the image of a panther that came to mind.

Deliberately Lacey focused on the photographs of current men's clothing in front of her. She had better things to do than to try to sort out conflicting impressions of Jed Merlin. Their association was doomed to be brief and she had the feeling both would be relieved when it was over.

Forty minutes later Armand, chicly attired in the glittering, sequined "suit of lights" worn by all the salon personnel, burst through the waiting-room door. He was waving the blow-dryer in his left hand as if it were a piece of Flash-Gordon–type artillery and he had just landed on a hostile planet.

"He is impossible!" the stylist raged at Lacey, who slowly got to her feet. "Utterly impossible! We got through that atrocious beard and I managed to get in a decent cut, but after that—" Black mane flying and dark eyes snapping, Armand sailed off into a string of foreign expletives that Lacey couldn't recognize. She doubted whether the stylist could either, given the fact that he'd been born and raised in California. But it sounded impressive.

"Calm down, Armand," she soothed, patting the shoulder of his dapper bolero jacket. "What seems to be the trouble? Isn't Jed cooperating? He promised he—"

"I'm cooperating. Up to a point."

Lacey stared at the stranger who was sauntering coolly

32

out of the salon, running a comb through tawny, sun-streaked hair. *Panther,* she thought as a chilling sensation shot down her spine. It was followed almost immediately by a rush of heat. Instantly she fought back both unwarranted emotions. Her nerves were playing strange tricks on her.

Wordlessly she watched as Jed Merlin came to a halt in front of the gilt-framed mirror, ducked his head slightly to see what he was doing, and casually flicked the small comb through the thickness of his hair. In the mirror her hazel eyes met his.

"Just keep that character with the blow-dryer away from me," he ordered calmly.

"You see? You see what I had to put up with?" Armand waved the dryer threateningly as he turned to Lacey for moral support. "How can I be expected to deal with this sort of lower-class impudence? You send him to me for style, for that *au courant* image which only I can achieve, and this is how he reacts!"

"I'm ready to go, Lacey," Jed announced, shoving the comb into his back pocket and turning to face her. "As I said before, take me or leave me."

Lacey blinked, realizing belatedly she was still staring. But she couldn't help it. Every hint of strength she'd seen in his body—the hardness she thought she'd glimpsed in the tawny eyes and the steel she'd caught once or twice in his voice—were both there in his face.

Hard-edged planes, a fierce blade of a nose thrown into prominence now that the beard had been removed, and a lean, aggressive jawline composed a face which would never be remotely handsome. One didn't use words like handsome and good-looking to describe that kind of blatant masculinity, Lacey thought dazedly. The boy of twenty had more than fulfilled his physical potential.

Aware of Armand's state of high dudgeon as well as a need to break her own sense of fascination, Lacey forced herself to step forward and take charge of the hostile situation.

"No, no, Armand, this is perfect. Absolutely right for him. You were a genius to stop when you did!"

Armand stared at her as Lacey slowly walked around Jed, examining every detail of the haircut. For his part, Jed stood so submissively still that Lacey knew he was silently mocking her. Irked with the implied derision, she reached out a hand and ran long, brilliantly shaded fingertips through the gold and brown of his hair.

"You've outdone yourself, Armand," she purred enthusiastically. "No one but you would have had the intelligent sense of style to realize that with that nose and that chin a blow-dry would have been all wrong. Much too soft."

There was a murmur of agreement among the various other occupants of the waiting room and Armand picked up on it at once. He lifted his chin proudly.

"Get me out of here," Jed snapped out of the side of his mouth.

"In a minute," she hissed back. "Try and behave for a little while longer!"

"Well, of course, it was a risk," Armand allowed. "I wasn't sure it was quite what you wanted. I mean these days everyone assumes one must have the carefully tousled look and you had specified something trendy."

"Armand, you should have known I'd trust your judgment. This is quite, quite perfect. I couldn't be happier."

34

Lacey stepped back, nodding. She ignored the metallic glitter in the slanting glance Jed threw at her.

"Good, good, I'm glad you're pleased," the stylist said with a gracious inclination of his head. "It is a pleasure to work with someone who appreciates talent!" He cast a meaningful eye around the plush waiting room, daring anyone there to deny his ability. No one did, of course. And no one would argue with him later when he told them what hairstyle was needed. Lacey wondered privately how many patrons would be going out the door that afternoon with Armand's latest "style."

It was another ten minutes before Lacey managed to get Jed free of his admirers. Even as she edged him toward the door she had a mental vision of herself trying to handle a jungle cat with only a piece of string tied around his neck. There was no reason to think Jed would do anything too drastic, was there? Still the thought of his losing his patience and taking a casual swipe at the nearest of Armand's patrons in the sort of offhand, totally devastating manner of an irritated panther was enough to hurry her steps.

They were nearly out the door when one final voice rose above the string of excited comments.

"It's got something, you know?" A young man with tightly curled blond hair remarked knowledgeably. "A kind of natural machismo look. And with those jeans and boots!"

Lacey saw the sudden laughter in Jed's eyes and she instinctively knew it would hit the taut line of his mouth in another second.

"Forget it," she gritted in an effort to forestall the inevitable. "Clayton knows I'm no more attracted to cowboys than I am to hippie gurus!"

"Do you always stereotype your men?" Jed asked with a mockingly polite interest.

"Why not? Men seem to fit so nicely into neat little categories!"

"And we're so flexible, aren't we?" he drawled in a too-casual manner that caused Lacey to eye him suspiciously. "I mean," he went on innocently, "here you are changing me from anti-establishment dropout to cowboy and, not satisfied with that, on to something else. Who else, Lacey?"

"To someone who looks like he could sweep me off my feet!" she snapped waspishly, beginning to feel a little goaded.

"You don't think I could manage that little maneuver on my own?"

"Don't be ridiculous! No offense, Jed, but you and I don't share what people would call compatible life-styles!" The short, dashing nut-brown hair danced lightly in the bright sun as Lacey shook her head with great certainty.

"Haven't you heard that opposites attract?"

"Even if that were true, and frankly I've always had doubts about it, Rick Clayton wouldn't believe it for an instant!" she shot back, slanting him a covert glance. It was impossible to keep from looking at him, she realized. Probably nothing more than the usual interest one had in someone whose appearance had changed in a matter of moments, she told herself.

"Is it so crucial that this Clayton believe you've been carried off by a wealthy, irresistible male?" Jed sounded

36

irritated again, his brief humor disappearing as he returned to the main subject.

"Yes," she retorted stonily, "it is. Rick understands about the attraction of money and . . . and sheer *flash*. He could comprehend a woman like me being swept off her feet by someone who offered more of both than he did!"

She thought Jed's response came through slightly gritted teeth. "He might comprehend it, but what does that say about you, Lacey, love?"

"Nothing you'd approve of, I'm sure," she snapped, and then wondered why his implied attack on her values had stung her so effectively. Let him think the worst. What did she care? As long as he played his part and played it well. "Let's just make sure that Rick thinks he 'discovered' my two-timing almost as soon as it began. He'll move quickly to break off the relationship first. He'll want that satisfaction. Being one up on everyone and everything is all that's important to Rick," she concluded with a trace of bitterness.

"If this guy's got the money and flash you claim attracts you, why are you so eager to dump him?" There was a chill in the panther's growl of a voice.

"That's my business," Lacey informed him brusquely, taking his arm to steer him into a men's clothing shop. "Just stop fretting, will you?"

"What are we doing in here?" he demanded aggressively, glancing around the interior of the exclusive store. The elegant displays featured the latest in European, Japanese, and New York fashions.

"This is the next step in the process of turning you into the kind of man I need. Stop complaining, for heaven's sake!"

37

"Stop complaining! This is going to cost me a fortune," he told her in a low, heated tone as a slim, elegant salesman came forward.

"Think of all the money you're saving by not having to pay off the complete debt!"

Lacey's eyes glittered with meaning as she smiled pointedly, and then she was turning to confront the salesman.

"May I be of service?" the man intoned, eyeing Jed's denims with a vaguely appalled expression.

"You may," Lacey declared heartily, taking charge with a vengeance. "We need your assistance in dressing my friend here up to his, shall we say, full potential? Ignore the jeans, they're going into the garbage. If you will be so kind as to give us the benefit of your expertise? I was thinking of one of the Italian designers. He has the body for it, don't you agree?"

Lacey and the salesman both scanned Jed's lithe frame as he stood with arrogant disgust in the middle of the expensive oriental carpet. The tawny eyes flared as he watched Lacey's perusal, but other than a low, mildly savage four-letter word, he said nothing.

"I believe you are absolutely right, madam," the salesman affirmed with a short, satisfied nod. "One of the Italian collections or, perhaps, a New York designer who has modified the lean look a little. There is a certain breadth to the shoulders that might not be easily accommodated by the European look."

"Excellent. We'll put ourselves in your hands," Lacey smiled, eyes lighting with laughter as she saw the frustrated dismay in Jed's expression. "Go along with the nice man, Jed," she instructed in deliberately syrupy tones, patting the smoothly muscled shoulders the salesman had noted. "And remember, I want to see everything before you make any decision."

"Would you care to step into the dressing room with me?" he invited a little too gently, tawny gaze full of a promise of retribution.

"I don't think that will be necessary. The light is stronger out here, and I'll be able to get a better view, don't you think?" She shouldn't be teasing him like this, Lacey told herself. After all, she needed his active cooperation. But there was an exhilarating recklessness about prodding the beast. Or was she unconsciously getting even with him for having turned down her proposal so long ago?

"Some other time, perhaps," he drawled, turning away to stalk after the elegant salesman.

Lacey's mouth broadened in amusement. Was he threatening her with delayed revenge? Perhaps before this was all over, he'd thank her!

The next half hour proved something of a struggle. Jed adamantly refused to even consider the dynamic current styles the salesman showed him. Nor did he obey Lacey's instructions to show her everything before he made his decisions.

"Jed, I want to see that suede jacket on you!" she tried calling out down the aisle of fitting rooms.

"Then you can damn well come in here and look at it," he called back in a tone of voice that clearly indicated he had no intention of modeling.

"I have a right to see what you're choosing!"

"Trust me," he murmured drily.

"I'm warning you," she grumbled, "if I don't like the final look, we're going to go through the whole scene again!"

"Don't worry, you're going to love the final look!"

It was going to be another case of "take me or leave me," Lacey realized in annoyance. She could put her faith only in the fact that nothing he chose from a store like this would be too terrible. Glumly she watched the salesman scurrying to and fro.

At long last the fitting-room door swung open and Jed emerged, straightening the collar of an open-throated yellow shirt. He was wearing it with a new pair of jeans. Automatically Lacey opened her mouth to protest, but he cut across her irritation with a casual warning.

"Be reasonable, Lacey. I'm going to be stuck with these clothes long after I've outlived my usefulness to you. I refuse to wind up with a bunch of high-gloss things I'll never wear. Besides, remember what the general consensus was back there at the hairstyling salon. The natural, macho look is *in*!" He threw her an unrepentant grin as he prepared to pay for the parcels the salesman was carrying over to the cashier.

He did look good, Lacey decided with a flash of artistic honesty. The yellow shirt was of excellent quality and had the proper California nonchalance, with a fit that was just snug enough across his broad shoulders. Everyone wore jeans, regardless of financial status. Somehow on Jed everything did look right, Lacey couldn't deny it. There was an air of sheer male toughness about him that would have made a mockery of some of the softer, trendier designs.

Biting her tongue on the words of reproach, Lacey followed him over to the cashier. "Did you get something decent for evening?" she demanded.

"Don't worry, madam," the salesman assured her

before Jed could respond. "I think that, on the whole, you'll be quite pleased. Not precisely what you or I might have chosen, but I believe it all works. We're fortunate that Mr. Merlin has a certain natural style that is well suited to the more casual, conservative look."

"A certain natural, macho style, would you say?" Jed inquired with a taunting that seemed to go unnoticed by everyone except Lacey.

"That sums it up rather well," the salesman agreed politely. "Will there be anything else?"

"I think that will do it," Jed told him, writing out the check. He collected the packages, piling several of them cheerfully into Lacey's arms, and led the way out the door.

As Lacey followed him to where her white Audi was parked at the curb, she had the distinct impression she was losing control of the situation.

"I'm getting hungry," Jed announced, taking the keys from her hand to open the trunk while Lacey stood holding packages. "What's for dinner? Or doesn't food and lodging come with the deal?"

She eyed him warily. "You're welcome to have dinner with me this evening," she told him formally as he took the packages one by one from her arms and stashed them in the trunk. "It will give us a chance to discuss my plans in more detail."

"Thank you, I accept," he said silkily. "But if I have to eat off black china, I'm going to insist we stop at the store for some paper plates first!"

"The china is white," she told him icily. "Now, if you'll kindly give me the keys, we can be on our way."

"That's all right," he grinned easily, tossing the keys into the air and catching them. "I'll drive."

41

With a man like this, Lacey decided in sudden intuition, a woman had to pick and choose her battles, because she couldn't win them all. Her mouth twisting wryly with that knowledge, she climbed into the passenger seat without protesting. If Jed wanted to battle L.A. traffic, why shouldn't she let him do exactly that? And the man always had been inordinately single-minded when he set his mind on something!

For some reason she thought about the way he'd tossed the keys into the air, catching them with easy certainty. The small action had a familiarity about it which once again brought back memories. Jed had come out onto the veranda of his father's house, tossing a set of keys in just that manner and indulgently announced he was going to take her swimming over on the nearby Santa Cruz beach. Lacey frowned, shaking off the memory of the happy day. Was he merely indulging her once more today by agreeing to her strange requests? She didn't like the notion. It was far more reassuring to believe herself in control of the situation rather than have the feeling she was being indulged.

"Stop slanting me those assessing little sidewise glances," Jed ordered, deftly moving the Audi out into Rodeo Drive traffic. "If you want to look at me, go ahead and take an honest look. Will I do or won't I?"

Goaded, Lacey openly studied his hard profile. "I think you'll do."

"I'm so relieved."

With a bland arrogance Lacey was forced to admire, he asserted his right to some road space between a red Ferrari and a black Jaguar. Jed seemed totally unintimidated by either vehicle.

"How did you get hold of Jackson, anyway?" he asked mildly.

"Your lawyer? His name was given to me by your father's bank. I got the bank's name from some old papers of my father's," she explained, her mind on her future plans once more. "I reminded him of the debt and told him what I wanted in exchange for not pressing for the money. He implied he would pass the information along to Merlin. I assumed, of course, that meant your father."

"And you thought the next thing to show up on your doorstep would be the tall, dark male commissioned by my father to meet your, er, needs," Jed concluded. "Instead you got me."

"Which brings up the interesting question of why you?" she shot back sweetly. "Why didn't you simply instruct your lawyer to find a suitable candidate?"

"Are you implying I'm unsuitable? Or am I simply not proving amenable enough?" He grinned, glancing at her.

"I was merely curious," she responded stiffly.

"The reason you got me instead of the hired help is that I prefer to pay my family debts in person," he condescended to inform her. "But if you're worrying about my lack of height . . ."

"Forget it, I'll wear flat-heeled shoes! I did it for my senior prom, and I can do it for you!"

"Thank you for the offer, but you needn't go to the trouble of changing your normal shoe style for my sake," he chuckled.

"You're not intimidated by taller women?" she inquired drily.

"There are other ways of dominating a woman besides towering over her," Jed said with unnerving assurance.

43

"And I'm blessed with all that natural machismo style, remember? Now that you've made me over into the proper image, you'll be putty in my hands."

"Are you trying to tell me that I'm going to suffer the same fate as Dr. Frankenstein? Ruined by my own creation?"

"No, no, no!" He laughed outright. "What we have here is more a case of the Pygmalion effect, I think. Like Henry Higgins in *My Fair Lady,* you're turning me into someone you really can fall for. Should be interesting to see what happens, hmmm? Not many women get the chance to recreate the romantic fantasy of their youth!"

For a split second Lacey simply stared at him, uncertain of just how much he was truly teasing her. Surely that wasn't downright unadulterated masculine arrogance she was hearing? Or was it? Did he really think there was a chance she'd get caught up in her own game? Perhaps he did. After all, Jed Merlin couldn't have any way of knowing how very serious this game was.

"Don't hold your breath," she advised caustically. "I have no intention of getting myself seduced by a man who prefers to wear a beard, sloppy jeans, and cowboy boots!" *Even if he does handle a car with the reflexes of a professional racing driver,* she added in silent acknowledgment of his skill at the wheel. She wasn't about to admit it aloud, but she found that skill soothing. It gave her a sense of being safe and protected. An illusion, she told herself, but nevertheless it was somewhat reassuring to recall that Jed Merlin had always been coolly competent in any situation in which he found himself.

"The beard's gone, the jeans now have a designer label sewn onto the back pocket, and the shirt cost over fifty dollars. Furthermore, I grew up on that estate you seem to remember so vividly. I can act the part you want. My father saw to it I had a well-rounded education," he told her with lazy amusement.

"Pity you didn't take advantage of that education to make something of your life," Lacey said pointedly, unable to resist the dig. She did not like the growing hint of indulgence she sensed in him!

"Does it matter what I choose to do with my own life as long as I have the Merlin money to draw upon?" he growled, his eyes on the heavy traffic.

"There is no excuse for being downright irresponsible with one's life, regardless of how well cushioned it happens to be," Lacey lectured.

"Do I hear a note of the Protestant work ethic in your voice?" he mocked. "I'd hardly call what you've done with your life responsible!"

She narrowed her eyes as she swung her head around sharply. "Don't tell me you're going to have the audacity to find fault with my life-style! At least I work for a living!"

"You mean you skim along the surface of a superficial, flashy world that has no use for commitment or genuine meaning. All that counts is being successful, on top of the latest fad, and living life with the right Los Angeles image."

"At least that gives us skimmers some goals in life," she parried.

"What do you take seriously, Lacey?" Jed asked as if intellectually interested in analyzing her answer.

"Probably none of the same things you do. Don't forget

to turn left at the next stoplight." She ignored the fact that he had already switched to the proper lane.

"My sense of direction happens to be fairly well developed."

Lacey blinked at the unexpected growl in his voice. Some men didn't take kindly to directions from a woman, she reflected with an inner smile. It was a pity, because she was so good at giving them.

"You can leave your packages in the trunk," she advised a few minutes later as Jed parked the Audi in the underground garage of Lacey's fashionable apartment building. "No sense hauling them all inside and then back again when you leave this evening."

"Why would I be leaving this evening?" Jed slammed the car door on his side and smiled across the roof with polite innocence. "I'm here to compromise you, remember? In any event, I haven't got reservations anywhere in town. I came straight from the airport to your apartment."

"We'll find a hotel room somewhere," Lacey sighed in resignation. "Come on."

"You never did tell me what's for dinner," Jed prompted as he followed her obediently into the elevator.

"Cracked crab and artichokes," she told him in a businesslike tone. "I'll put on the artichokes while you start phoning for a hotel room."

"It seems to me the least you could do for an old family friend is put him up for the night!"

"Given the fact that I haven't seen you since I was thirteen years old, you hardly qualify as an old family friend. The phone is over there beside that black glass vase."

"You're probably one of the few people left in the civilized world with a black phone. But it does go with the rest of this weird decor."

"I'll make a deal with you. Refrain from making nasty comments about my life-style and my apartment, and I'll return the favor," Lacey ordered.

"You certainly developed in a consistent fashion. Even as a kid you were bossy! All right, all right, now is as good a time as any to start demonstrating how well I can carry out the role of urbane, wealthy seducer."

"Just practice the urbane and wealthy part," Lacey told him as she disappeared into the all-white kitchen. "I have no interest in the seduction techniques you probably perfected in some sleazy commune!"

He came to the kitchen doorway and lounged against the frame with a self-confidence that irritated her. There was a distinctly wicked gleam in the gold and brown eyes as he smiled deliberately.

"You seem to forget, I won't be using the sleazy commune-style techniques. I'm paying off a debt, and I shall endeavor to give you your money's worth."

"Go make your telephone calls," she ordered imperiously, running water into a kettle for the artichokes.

"You'll see," he promised, turning away to obey her injunction. "You won't be able to resist me. After all, I'm going to be your ideal man!"

Lacey hid her grin until he was safely out of sight. She hadn't bargained on working with someone who had a sense of humor. The whole project had seemed so serious when she'd first embarked upon it. Somehow having Jed around was taking the dangerous edge off the matter. Like the time he'd given her surfing lessons, she recalled wryly.

She'd been terrified of the high waves and the fragile support of the board, but Jed's easy humor and assured skill had soon made her forget her fears. Perhaps it had only been her overactive imagination that had gotten her into this current mess.

Was that all it was? A case of overreaction to an essentially meaningless conversation she'd overheard? But she was afraid to take the risk. Rick Clayton had managed to frighten her, and she wanted out of the relationship that had been developing between them. And she wanted out in a way that wouldn't alert him to the possibility that she knew more than she should about his import-export business.

But Jed Merlin was turning out to be a complication for which she hadn't bargained. Well, if nothing else, he would help take her mind off the dark imaginings she had been prone to lately. She'd been afraid to discuss the matter with anyone else.

"The occasion calls for a glass of wine, don't you think?" Jed demanded a few minutes later as he wandered back into the kitchen. "Something white, dry, reasonably assertive, and a tad fruity. Where do you store the stuff?"

"On the bottom shelf of the refrigerator. Here's the opener." Lacey smiled politely as she handed it to him. "Trying to impress me with your well-rounded education?"

"Just trying to do my job, ma'am. Just trying to do my job."

He opened the wine with an aplomb that indicated it wasn't a novelty for him to handle expensive bottles of Chardonnay. But, then, why should it be? Lacey frowned slightly as she lifted the glass he'd poured for her. Just because Jed had opted out of upper-class opulence somewhere along the line didn't mean he'd never experienced it. It was confusing, she decided as she sipped the pale gold wine. It was complicated keeping this man in his proper box. He had a way of shuttling back and forth across the stereotypes before her very eyes. And none of the neat categories quite fit.

"I'm glad you didn't carry the black decor on into the kitchen," he was saying. His gaze roved the white-on-white, highly functional room. "At least there's a place to escape to when the front room gets intolerable."

Lacey's mouth quirked upward as she set down her wineglass and began unwrapping the cooked, cracked crab. "Come back in six months and you won't recognize the place."

"Six months?"

"I change it every six months," she explained patiently. "My apartment is one of my chief selling tools. I redo it frequently so that prospective clients can get a feel for my style and for what is currently 'in.'"

"Isn't it a little exhausting having to live your whole life on the wake of whatever happens to be current?" There was a genuine note of curiosity in the question, and Lacey found herself answering it seriously.

"I think of it as part of my job. And there's a certain pleasure in being able to play around so much with design. Redoing my apartment or someone else's is probably akin to what an artist feels when he or she paints a new picture. I like changing my environment."

"And your men?"

"Oh, I change them much more frequently than I

change my apartment!" she snapped, her indulgence fading as she caught the taunting look in his eyes.

"Well, at least you're honest about it," he observed, his mouth tightening. "Got someone lined up to take Clayton's place after you've collected the diamond pendant?"

"As a matter of fact, no." Lacey arranged the cracked crab in an artistic design on the plate, adding wedges of lemon and little bowls of sauce. Every time she began to find Jed Merlin amusing, he switched into his annoying mode. She picked up the tray and turned to find him standing directly behind her.

The tawny eyes were narrowed with masculine assessment and a sudden wave of sensual danger lapped at her. He didn't move for a moment, yet Lacey was overwhelmingly aware of his supple strength. Once again he seemed to have crossed invisible boundaries, transforming himself from a mocking, casually disapproving counter-culture type into something far more menacing: a male who was beginning to make it clear he was discovering an interesting challenge in her.

As soon as he saw the wariness in her eyes, Jed's expression relaxed into one of devilish amusement. Reaching out, he gallantly took the tray from her hands.

"Who would have guessed that paying off my father's debt would have been so intriguing?" he murmured.

# CHAPTER THREE

"Well? Do you think I'll do?" Jed smiled across the short expanse of the black glass dining table, leaning forward in the chrome and leather Breuer chair to prop his elbow on the surface. The smile was another of the faintly teasing, faintly wicked, enormously charming ones he had been using on Lacey all through dinner. A smile she dimly remembered.

"Yes," she replied honestly. "I think you'll do very well. You can be a very pleasant companion when you put your mind to it, can't you?" She tried to look at him as if he were a rather amusing example of an interesting species. It was difficult and getting more so, trying to maintain a businesslike distance between them. Jed Merlin was meshing a little too easily into the role she had outlined. He was quite deliberately turning himself into the kind of man she found so attractive.

"When the inspiration is sufficient, I can manage quite a few things." The smile had moved into his eyes, where it blended with another expression—one that had been making Lacey very aware of him. It also made her curiously edgy. She felt a need to hold her own against him.

"What are you going to do if you develop a taste for the

51

superficial, trendy style of life, Jed?" she taunted lightly, swirling the last of the wine in her glass. "Will you be content to go back to your antiestablishment ways?"

He rose, collecting the white plates and a handful of silverware. "I'm a firm believer in the value of acquiring a variety of experiences, but I try not to become addicted to anything," he murmured.

"Anything or anyone?" she pressed, following him back into the kitchen. Even as she said the words she could not have explained why she had deliberately asked the provocative question.

He glanced back at her over his shoulder as he placed the dishes in the sink. The tawny eyes darkened with a touch of flame. "Any*thing,*" he stressed coolly. "Unlike you, I don't have any preconceived prejudices against meaningful commitments."

"I'll bet you don't," she shot back silkily. "In fact, I'll bet you've had a vast number of 'meaningful commitments' in your life. Perhaps more than one at the same time! Don't try to condemn my life-style, Jed, when we both know yours is no better. In fact, I'd say yours is less honest than mine because it uses all sorts of euphemisms to describe what is essentially a very free and easy approach to commitments of any kind."

He swung around on his heel, leaning back against the sink, and folding his arms consideringly across his chest. "You think you know all about my life, don't you?" he challenged gently.

Lacey stood quite still, her head tipped slightly to one side as she endured his bold gaze. "As much as you seem to know about mine," she retorted.

"Perhaps," he suggested, lowering his arms and striding

slowly toward her, "we both should learn a bit more about each other before we hurl any more accusations, hmmm?"

Lacey knew the stroke of the tawny eyes was as much a deliberate caress as the touch of his hands would have been. She should have moved away from it just as she would have moved out of reach if he'd tried to take hold of her.

But she didn't. A deep, feminine curiosity that had been growing steadily throughout the evening held her still for the crucial moment it took for Jed to approach within touching distance. Did a panther first hypnotize his prey? she wondered, intrigued.

"I have discovered," Jed purred in a dark, velvety voice, "a desire to learn more about what makes a woman like you tick."

"Sociological studies, Jed?" she whispered, strangely captivated by the man who had emerged from behind the beard and faded jeans. What was Jed Merlin really like? All evening the categories and stereotypes had been blurring. Now she had before her a man who seemingly fit neatly into an exceedingly attractive niche. It was an effort to remind herself he was merely playing a role.

"My favorite subject," he agreed, the edge of his mouth curving in gentle humor. He lifted his hands slowly, giving her plenty of opportunity to twist aside. When she didn't, the long, strong fingers settled at the side of her throat, thumbs under her chin.

She should have turned aside, Lacey told herself. She ought to have stepped nimbly, lightly, firmly out of reach. But the strange sense of being ensnared was stronger than the inner warnings. He was going to kiss her. Was that so earth-shattering? Of course not. And he had been a most interesting, most attractive companion this evening. Besides, she added silently as his fingers began to burn her skin, he was doing her something of a favor. What could one kiss hurt? As a young girl she'd wondered. . . .

And so the entrapment was a reality, aided and abetted by the willing victim who refused to perceive the reckless danger in the situation. Lacey waited, lips slightly parted, a deep look of curiosity and invitation in her hazel eyes. The moment seemed fraught with a breathless anticipation that was entirely out of character with the nature of the kiss, but she couldn't take time to analyze the matter. Not just then.

Slowly, as if stepping carefully into unfamiliar territory, Jed closed the small gap between them, angling his head slightly and taking her lips with a warm, exploratory movement. The fingers stroked on the side of her throat lightly, provocatively as he molded her mouth beneath his own.

For a long moment Lacey stood passively beneath the soft assault, letting her emotions sort out their responses to this man who had captivated them so easily this evening. She saw him now with a woman's emotions, not a child's.

When the gentle exploration began to slip over the edge into masculine persuasion, Lacey's body softened in reaction. Jed must have felt it because his sensitive hands slid down, gliding over her shoulders, along her arms, and finally around her waist. When his palms flattened, urging her closer, Lacey obeyed unthinkingly. Her arms lifted to encircle his neck.

"There is something to be said for a similarity in

54

height," he husked against her lips, crowding her more tightly against the hard leanness of his body.

Lacey looked at him through her lowered lashes, a sensual humor etching her smile. "No cricks in the neck from bending over too far?"

"Among other factors," he whispered, nuzzling the lobe of her ear with lazy interest. "You fit nicely too." As if to demonstrate, he slid his hands upward to the nape of her neck and then slowly, tantalizingly brought them down the length of her back to her hips. En route he seemed to meld every inch of her intimately against him.

When Lacey caught her breath as the feel of his body asserted itself, he curved his fingers heavily into her rounded bottom. Small shivers of fiery excitement shot hungrily up into the pit of her stomach.

"Jed?" The soft moan was half plea, half encouragement. Lacey was almost unaware the sound had issued from her throat as she shut her eyes against the rush of sensation.

"Relax, sweetheart," he told her in that dark panther's purr. "I'm not going anywhere. We've got all evening."

All evening? But she was too involved to question his exact meaning. His mouth was trailing slow, heated little kisses from the base of her ear, along the line of her jaw, and back up to her lips. She awaited the impact of his mouth on hers with an eagerness that would amaze her later.

There was no swooping capture, though, only a tiny, gentle nibbling at the edge of her softened lower lip. She felt the hint of his teeth and then the tip of his tongue as he outlined the shape of her mouth.

Of their own volition her fingers began to knead the

smooth contours of his back, finding the length of his spine and following it down to where it disappeared beneath the line of his jeans. When he groaned beneath her touch, she took a strange pleasure in having elicited the response.

"Oh!" The exclamation was forced from her as strong fingers on her hips suddenly sank very deeply. The sound was almost immediately cut off as he ceased the subtle teasing of her mouth and sealed it completely with his own.

This time there was a new element in the kiss. Almost at once his tongue plunged aggressively into the honeyed darkness behind her teeth, seeking to drink the essence of what waited there. Instinctively, perhaps a little defensively, Lacey's fingers raked the line of his waist as she adjusted to the new onslaught.

"Are you going to leave your mark on me, witch?" he grated against her mouth as he half-broke the heavy contact.

"Is a sorcerer of Merlin's caliber afraid of a mere witch?" she countered huskily.

"I probably should be," he muttered ruefully. "If I had any sense, I would be."

"Life is full of risks, even for a magician in jeans."

"What do you know about risks, lady?" he growled. "I have the feeling you've never taken any real ones, not the kind that put your whole being in jeopardy!"

She heard the faint accusation in his voice and stirred in his arms.

"Am I going to get another lecture on the nature of a true commitment?"

"No," he responded roughly, holding her still. "Not tonight. I don't seem to be able to find my lecture notes."

This time when he took control of her mouth he used his tongue to seek out and engage hers in a duel from which she could not escape. Lacey trembled against him and she sensed his satisfaction. When next he lifted his head, there was a golden fire deep in the tawny eyes.

Without a word he cradled her against the length of him and guided her gently out of the kitchen. In a warm dreamy haze Lacey allowed herself to be led toward the black leather couch. Jed sank down on it, pulling her after him so that she was lying nestled across his hard thighs.

Holding her securely, he began to feather the delicate, unexpected places—the tip of her nose, the little spot behind her ear, the fringes of her lashes. Each place he touched with his lips was left sensitized, charged with a tingling electricity that fed into the growing whirlpool of desire.

When his fingertips touched the pulse at the base of her throat, Lacey's toes curled tightly and one sandal fell to the dark granite floor with a faint sound. She sighed heavily against his mouth, and when she tried to recover the breath, the blue and red of her jumpsuit bodice seemed to part. He worked his way down the embroidered fastenings with a slow inevitability which built the sense of anticipation and desire to a higher and more demanding pitch. It was unlike anything she'd ever known before. Everything about Jed Merlin was different—strangely, compellingly exciting.

Instead of sophisticated expertise, he touched her with a sensitive, exploring wonder. Instead of masculine arrogance, Jed kissed her with an honest need that was far more seductive. And instead of the feeling that he was merely another male out for what he could get, Lacey had the sensation of being caressed by a magician who had an innate respect for a woman's power.

And ultimately the combination was infinitely more seductive than the shallow, polished performance of other men. When Jed slid his hand inside the collar of the unbuttoned jumpsuit, Lacey couldn't bring herself to protest. Her nails dug into the thickness of his hair and she moaned as he found the curve of her full breast.

"You fill my hand perfectly," he muttered thickly as she buried her face in the curve of his neck. His thumb rasped gently across the rosy tip of one nipple, drawing it forth. "And you respond so beautifully."

Delicately, giving in to the unbearable need to vent her rising excitement, Lacey sank her teeth into the tanned shape of his neck. She heard his muffled exclamation of response and it encouraged her to probe beneath the edge of his open shirt collar.

When she fumbled with the first button, he tightened his cradling hold, and the fingers at her breast squeezed enticingly. She gasped and nearly tore off the next button.

The warm chuckle deep in his chest added to her growing impatience, and when she found the curling cloud of tawny brown hair on his chest, Lacey plunged her hand into it with unaccustomed greed.

"Who would have thought there was so much soft excitement under that sophisticated veneer?" Jed breathed into her hair. "You look at a man with such feminine disdain, such supreme confidence, and then you explode in his hands. What other secrets are you hiding, sweet witch? I want to learn them all!"

*Secrets?* Somehow the word clicked in her mind, freeing the ensorceled, rational side of her thoughts. Secrets. Yes, she had secrets. Dangerous secrets. She had no business forgetting their urgency just because this forgotten man had walked into her life and touched her with his magic.

No, she thought a little wildly as he pressed her gently back against the curve of his arm and bent his head to her throat. He hadn't walked into her life, she had deliberately brought him into it. She had unwittingly conjured up a sorcerer in her search for assistance and now she must maintain control over him or risk . . . Risk what? Surely she could handle a bohemian maverick who made no pretense of his disapproval of her values and her life.

"Jed, Jed, that's enough . . ."

"I'm not sure I can get enough of you tonight," he growled as he kissed the slope of her breast. His hand flattened beneath its fullness, trailing down to the contour of her stomach. "No matter how much you give me!"

She drew in her breath. "I'm not, that is, I'm not going to give you anything! Please, Jed, this has gone far enough!"

Slowly he lifted his head and stared down into her anxious face. "Don't play games with me, Lacey," he warned.

She moved restlessly, aware of the tautness in his thighs and the strength in the arm that held her so closely. "I'm not playing games, Jed. I never meant this to happen, and I'm going to put a stop to it. We have a—a business relationship and I—"

"I'd hardly call it business," he murmured, his mouth twisting wryly. "But even if it were, what has that got to do with this?" As if to emphasize what he meant by *this*, he stroked a hand along her side from shoulder to thigh

59

and his eyes moved hungrily from her face to her breasts. "Are you afraid to find yourself wanting me?"

"Of course I'm not afraid of you," she snapped, struggling to sit up. He let her fumble to an upright position and she raked a hand through her short, bouncy hair in what she hoped was a casual motion. "I'm simply telling you that this has gone far enough. I didn't send for you just to have you seduce me. We've already agreed you're not my type!"

"Still worried about the fact that I'm not over six feet? Don't fret, darling, good things come in small packages." He grinned a wicked, slashing grin that promised much and dared even more.

"Jed!"

A little shaken by the gleaming threat of piracy in his eyes, Lacey scrambled off his lap and onto her feet, only to find herself standing awkwardly, one shoe off and one shoe on. Vastly annoyed with herself and with the entire situation, she kicked off the remaining sandal. It was easier than trying to put the other one back on her bare foot.

"I think it's time you left," she informed him loftily, clumsily fastening the opening of the jumpsuit and using the action as an excuse not to meet his eyes. She was aware of him getting lazily to his feet.

"Left for where?" he inquired interestedly. He made no move to redo the buttons of his new yellow shirt.

"For your hotel! Stop teasing me, Jed!" she scolded, frowning furiously.

"I wasn't the one doing the teasing this evening." He lifted her chin with his thumb and forefinger so that she was forced to meet his still-flickering eyes. "I don't play silly little games with near strangers!"

Lacey whitened beneath the insult. "Oh, no! You wouldn't play games with a near stranger, would you? You'd be quite happy to go to bed with one!"

His expression hardened. "You admit you were playing games with me, witch?"

"Don't put words in my mouth, damn it!" Hazel rage crackled suddenly in the depths of Lacey's eyes and her hands clenched into fists. "I allowed you a kiss after what had been a reasonably pleasant evening. You took advantage of the situation to try and get me into bed. I see no reason I should do any apologizing. You're the one who presumed too much on short acquaintance!"

"I didn't presume," he growled huskily, releasing her chin to slide his hand intimately around the nape of her neck. "I merely responded honestly to the situation. You seemed to want me, and I sure as hell wanted you. What was wrong with that? And ours is hardly a short acquaintance."

"Wrong with it? You're the one who's been lecturing me about commitments and meaningful relationships!" She refused to respond to his last comment.

"And have all my lectures sunk in already?" he mused, tugging her gently closer. "Are you asking for commitments and meaning, Lacey? Because if you are, such things take a little time. We have to start somewhere."

He was going to kiss her again! Firmly Lacey brought her hands up to wedge against his chest. Damn it! He wasn't more than an inch taller than she was, and she was hardly the delicate, fragile type. If push came to shove, she ought to be able to hold him at bay physically!

Jed halted his attempt to pull her back into his arms,

glancing reproachfully down at the fingertips digging into the fabric of his shirt.

"This is, I take it, an unequivocal rejection?"

"You're reading the situation correctly," Lacey gritted out. "I hope you're not going to be difficult?"

"Because if I am difficult, you're prepared to resort to force?" he concluded wryly.

Lacey said nothing, arching one eyebrow in silent confirmation. His hands fell away from her and he threw himself lithely back down onto the leather sofa. Leaning back, fists locked behind his head, Jed regarded her with coolly narrowed eyes.

"I wouldn't dream of engaging you in an outright battle. Think how embarrassing it would be if I lost," he mocked.

"Very hard on the masculine ego, I imagine."

"Very." He sighed deeply. "Well, where do I sleep?"

Lacey hesitated for a startled beat of time. "Your hotel, naturally," she finally ground out.

"Didn't I mention that I wasn't able to get a room when I phoned earlier?" He looked mildly surprised by his own negligence.

"Jed, I'm warning you!"

"What's the problem? I'm supposed to be compromising you, aren't I? Only you and I will know that we didn't share the same bed tonight," he added blandly.

"You're supposed to be doing it subtly!"

"There's nothing quite as convincing as a full-fledged affair," he told her loftily. "Having me stay the night is much more likely to condemn you in Clayton's eyes than simply being seen out with me in a few strategic night-spots. What's the matter? Are you afraid that if you go too far you might not get the diamond pendant? Just your walking papers?"

A heated flush stormed into Lacey's cheeks at the insolence. God! What he must think of her! Well, that wasn't her problem. She needed his assistance, but that didn't mean she had to defend all her actions to him.

"I'll see what I can do about getting you a room," she hissed, spinning around and heading toward the phone.

"Lacey, please!" The sudden, unexpected coaxing in his voice almost halted her. She sensed him getting to his feet and coming up behind her. "Let me stay the night. I'll sleep on that ridiculous black sofa, if you like, but don't send me out to a hotel. It's late, and I hate hotels!"

He slid his arms around her waist as she bent over the phone book, flipping it open. "What do you mean, you hate them?" she demanded bracingly. "What's wrong with hotel rooms, for heaven's sake?"

"I have a phobia about them," he confided, holding her lightly against him and inhaling the fragrance of her tousled hair. "Don't you have any phobias?"

Lacey's fingernail tapped against the Yellow Pages in annoyance. "You expect me to believe a flimsy story like that?"

"No," he sighed. "But being the man of your dreams, I was hoping I could get away with it!"

"The man of my dreams!" She twisted out of his arms to face him.

"Haven't I been the man you wanted this evening? Didn't I engage you in witty conversation over dinner? Display an appropriate knowledge of good wine and the latest films? Don't I look the part now that the beard is gone? Am I not an older version of the man to whom you once proposed?"

"Your sense of humor is a little misplaced!" She felt as if she were being cornered, and she didn't care for image one bit. The panther in him was too close to the surface. Lacey flung out a hand to indicate the listings in the phone book. "Find a hotel, Jed!"

"And if I refuse?" He smiled at her with a deceptive blandness which somehow managed to make her very wary.

"Then I shall throw you out the door and let you fend for yourself!"

"If you do, I'll return the favor," he promised softly.

That stopped her. "What are you talking about?" she whispered, wide-eyed.

He shrugged with a supreme lack of interest but there was metal in the brown and gold eyes. "Throw me out and I'll keep going. Back home."

"You can't! You owe me the help!"

"My father owed your father," he growled. "I don't owe you a dime and if you want to take it to court I'm probably better able to stand the costs than you are. Face it, Lacey, you need my willing cooperation in this and you know it. If you didn't know it, you'd be demanding the thirty thousand. I seriously doubt Clayton's diamond will be worth anywhere near that amount."

Lacey flinched, forcefully aware of the fact that in that moment the indulgence in him was at a dangerously low ebb.

She ground her teeth in disgust. He was quite right; she did need his help. He had no way of knowing just how badly she needed it! The diamond pendant Rick Clayton gave dismissed women friends with such casual flair meant nothing to her. She wanted the security of knowing he was no longer interested in her in any way.

Jed watched the worried look flicker across her face and he softened, the corner of his mouth kicking upward in gentle amusement. "It's all right, honey, I'll help you with your crazy project. But in turn I'd like a little trust. I won't lay a hand on you tonight if that's the way you want it. But I don't want to be sent packing to some hotel just because you've tired of the evening's fun and games!"

"It wasn't that way at all!" she protested, hurt in spite of herself by his assessment. "I never intended you to spend the night, Jed."

"When I first arrived earlier today, I never intended that either," he murmured. "But somehow during dinner it began to seem like a good idea."

"I don't see what major shifts occurred over the cracked crab," she complained heatedly.

"I got a chance to know you a little better," he smiled.

"You mean you decided you had a chance of getting a convenient bedmate for the night!"

"That," he drawled, "would have been a pleasant bonus, but it's not the reason I've decided to spend the night here."

"Then what is? You're just being difficult? Contrary? Trying to show me I don't hold the upper hand? Go on, Jed, tell me exactly why you're blackmailing me into letting you spend the night!" she flared.

He hesitated consideringly. "It's a bit hard to explain," he finally allowed.

"I'll bet it is! Especially after all those disapproving remarks about my shallow, superficial values."

"All of which still hold true," he grinned.

"Jed Merlin, I'm on the verge of losing my temper completely. I suggest you talk and talk fast, or you're going to be out the door, regardless of how badly I want your help!"

"Am I, Lacey?" He moved slightly, far enough to prop himself against the white wall, and his eyes roved over her form. "Are you really going to call my bluff? Throw me out in a fit of pique? Somehow I don't think so."

"You think I want that diamond pendant so badly I'll put up with your overbearing behavior?" she asked acidly, aware of a new wariness in her nervous system as she watched him carefully.

"Perhaps," he mused.

"Or do you believe I'm so attracted to the man I created this afternoon that I'll tolerate his arrogance?" she challenged.

"Perhaps."

"Of all the . . ." she began, outraged.

He cut off the angry flow of words with a purring growl. Quite suddenly the panther in him was very evident. "Or perhaps there's more to this situation than you've seen fit to explain, Lacey. Something about your little game doesn't ring true, honey, and I was always intrigued by interesting puzzles."

In the tense instant that followed his words, Lacey tried to hide the impact they'd had on her. What sort of wild guesses was he making about this whole mess?

The possibility of his perceiving more than she had ever

intended introduced a new factor into the equation and it alarmed her.

"The blankets," she told him with the hauteur of one who is trying to leave the battlefield with dignity intact, "are in the hall closet. You'll love them. They're black. So are the towels!"

# CHAPTER FOUR

It was the rattle of her white china that awakened Lacey the next morning. As she came slowly awake, her tired brain trying to figure out why she could hear the clatter of dishes when she herself was not in the kitchen and the bedroom door was thrust open.

She sat up abruptly with a sheet clutched to her throat in a classic pose. Her hazel eyes widened, framed by her sleep-tousled hair as she saw Jed come to a halt in the doorway.

He blinked lazily, taking in his surroundings with an air of obvious surprise. "You'll have to forgive me," he murmured, coming toward her with a cup and saucer in hand. "For a minute there I thought I'd accidentally walked into the wrong bedroom."

"You have," Lacey managed grimly. "Mine."

"If it's yours, I'm in the right place," he grinned unperturbably, placing the cup of steaming coffee down on the gilded nightstand. "But I'll admit I wouldn't have recognized it. I don't see a single touch of black!"

Automatically Lacey followed his gaze around the room she had designed with the inspiration of an English country house in mind. Sunny yellow walls reflected the

California light and the restrained flowered rug formed a backdrop to the four-poster bed with its whimsical carved parrots. More colorful birds graced the crewel quilt. One or two Chinese antiques anchored the lighter shades but Jed was right in his observation: There wasn't a hint of black.

"This room," Lacey declared with great emphasis, "is not a showroom! Being a house guest does not give you the entire run of the place, Jed. Will you please leave?"

"So this room is done the way you really want it, huh?" He looked vastly interested, fingering the quilt with an appraising touch. "Not as an example for potential clients?"

"Jed!"

His eyes swept over her nearly bare shoulders, taking in the thin straps of the low-cut peach satin of her nightgown. Lacey was infuriated with herself as she sensed the heat rising in her cheeks. Her eyes narrowing angrily, she opened her mouth to add another warning.

"It's okay, I'm going," he told her hastily. "Don't I even get any thanks for the coffee?"

"I don't know yet. I haven't tasted it!"

"It's the thought that counts," he reminded her from the door. Then he was out of the room, leaving Lacey with the fleeting impression of having had her English country garden briefly invaded.

He was waiting for her half an hour later when she emerged in a sleek gray skirt, a raspberry silk blouse with a large bow at the throat, and a soft, body-skimming black jacket. Glancing up from the morning paper he was perusing over his coffee, Jed shot Lacey an inquiring glance.

"I take it from the way you're dressed that we're not going to the beach?"

"I'm going into work for a few hours," she told him pointedly, sitting down at the table and reaching for the box of cereal he'd already put out. "I have an appointment with a client. You may do as you please, so long as you're available for dinner this evening. I like that shirt, by the way," she added grudgingly as she eyed the conservatively striped material.

He smiled benignly. "I thought you would. I chose it with you in mind."

"Just think of the wonderful new wardrobe you're going to have to show off to your friends," she retorted sweetly.

"They'll probably kick me out of the commune. When are you going to be home?"

"Around noon."

"And where are we going for dinner tonight?"

"A place over in Marina Del Rey. A lot of Rick's friends hang out there on the weekends," she said with outward calm.

"And you want to make certain we're seen, right?"

Lacey nodded and finished her cereal in near silence. It wasn't simply the increasing tension as her plans began to become reality that was making her edgy, she realized. It was Jed's unsettling presence. The intimacy over the breakfast table was unnerving, to say the least, although he seemed totally at ease. When the time came to leave for work, Lacey almost fled the apartment.

Indeed, her office, which was part showroom and part studio, seemed a welcome refuge that morning. With an eagerness born of a desire to temporarily forget her personal problems, Lacey prepared for the arrival of her client. By the time a somewhat apprehensive Mrs. Elizabeth Hadley walked through her door, Lacey was ready for her.

"Good morning, Mrs. Hadley! You're right on time. I'm looking forward to showing you some of the initial plans I've prepared. After that walk-through of your charming home last week, I came right back here and started putting together some ideas. I think you're going to love them!"

The forty-year-old conservatively dressed woman looked at Lacey with uncertain hope in her gray-green eyes. The Hadleys had only recently moved to the Los Angeles area from the Midwest, Mr. Hadley having accepted a position with an aerospace firm. The acclimatization to California was proving something of a challenge for the entire family, Lacey had quickly deduced, except for the teen-age children, who were apparently adapting beautifully.

"Did you really think our place was . . . was charming?" Elizabeth asked in ill-concealed surprise. "I mean, I know it's hardly modern or stylish. I was afraid you'd take one look at it and decide there was nothing you could do—"

"Have you ever worked with an interior designer before?" Lacey smiled understandingly.

"I'm afraid not. The home we had back in Kansas was the only one George and I had ever owned until this move west. We furnished it with the cheapest things we could find shortly after we were married and, although we added to and replaced occasionally down through the years, there was never an opportunity to really do it right. Now that we're in a position to start from scratch, I've convinced George to let me hire an expert . . ." Her voice trailed off uncertainly once again.

71

"And you're afraid I'll come up with something that will shock poor George to the core?" Lacey chuckled knowingly.

"Well, George comes from a long line of conservative farmers," Elizabeth confided, obviously grateful to have the hidden source of unease brought out into the open for honest discussion. "I started thinking after you left last week that perhaps I'd made a mistake."

"Mrs. Hadley, come and look at some of the designs and plans I've prepared," Lacey said cheerfully. "And stop looking so worried. Part of an interior designer's responsibility is to assess the psychological and emotional requirements of a family's life-style. I'm well aware of the fact that Los Angeles is proving a bit of a culture shock for you and George! I wouldn't dream of adding to that shock by doing something wild and dramatic to your home."

Elizabeth Hadley looked relieved. "Thank you for understanding. Every time I look around your shop here and see all these modern, artistic things, I worry that George would go crazy trying to live surrounded by them!"

"A lot of people would." Why did she suddenly think of Jed? Lacey pulled out her sketch pad with one hand and reached for a wallpaper sample book with the other. "The home should be a refuge for the family, not a showcase for visitors. It's true that some people want a showcase, and for them I do dramatic things that really would drive other people crazy. But for a real family like yours, I want to achieve an environment that is comfortable, yet something of which you can be proud."

Mrs. Hadley, growing rapidly more relaxed as Lacey began spreading out the warm quiet designs she'd prepared, began to smile and nod. "Yes, yes, George will like that arrangement near the fireplace. He's always been a pipe-and-slippers sort of man! And that kitchen is fabulous! I never would have thought of that center island idea. Kind of reminds me of an old farmhouse kitchen yet it looks so modern!"

"That's the trick in this case, Mrs. Hadley," Lacey said. "We want your family to feel comfortable, but we don't want everyone feeling they never really left the Midwest. Now, here are some wallpaper colors and textures I'd like to go over with you."

They spent another half hour assessing the various samples, and by the end of the session, not only did Elizabeth Hadley feel vastly more confident in her decision to use a designer, Lacey felt far more relaxed herself. There was nothing like work to take one's mind off one's problems, she thought wryly.

"I can't wait to show these sketches to George and the kids," Mrs. Hadley exclaimed as she prepared to leave.

Lacey saw her client out the door and then turned back to the worktable to gather up the various papers and samples lying there. The shop seemed very quiet now that Elizabeth Hadley was gone. Lacey sighed inwardly. It was almost noon. Time to go home. For the first time, she allowed herself to wonder if Jed Merlin had elected to disappear for the day or if she would find him waiting for her.

It wasn't until she had parked her Audi in the apartment garage and started up in the elevator that Lacey acknowledged to herself that she hoped she would find Jed waiting for her. And with that thought came the further realization that last night was the first good night's sleep she'd had since overhearing that conversation between Rick Clayton and one of his subordinates. There had been a sense of safety having a panther in the house, she told herself half-humorously as she put the key into the lock.

The tug of amusement that curved her lips faded to resignation as she took in the sight before her. There, sprawled across the black leather sofa, was her neighbor, Mona Hawkins, known to her many fans and loyal readers as Tanya Radcliffe.

Mona, her long red hair falling in sultry curls across the shoulders of her royal purple kimono, her green eyes vividly highlighted with burnished gold eyeshadow, and her long legs tantalizingly displayed, was well and truly in her Tanya role this morning, Lacey decided. Seated across from the exotic creature on the couch was Jed, who had apparently been listening intently to something Mona had been saying. Both of them glanced up in surprise as Lacey walked through the door.

"Don't let me interrupt anything," Lacey said coolly, tossing down her leather purse and keys. "I'll just disappear quietly into the kitchen. You won't even know I'm here!"

"Lacey, dear!" Mona drawled in that rich, vibrant voice she had perfected so well on various talk shows. "What's wrong? You look upset."

"It's nothing, Mona . . ."

"Mona?" Jed finally spoke, slanting an inquiring glance at the beautiful redhead on the couch.

"Sorry, *Tanya,*" Lacey amended lightly as she walked past the other two en route to the kitchen. Normally Mona's flamboyant ways didn't bother her, but for some reason it was incredibly irritating to walk in and find her luscious neighbor entertaining Jed.

"My, we're obviously feeling a trifle moody today, aren't we?" Mona asked with a superficial sympathy that was about as close to the real thing as she could convey. "I'd best be on my way. See you later, Lacey, and thanks for letting me meet your charming friend here. When you're through with him, pitch him across the hall, will you? I can always find a use for his sort!"

With a cheerful wave and a swirl of purple silk Mona was gone, leaving behind more than a trace of her expensive perfume. Lacey didn't see her go, but she heard the door shut as she opened the refrigerator and began scanning the contents for something that would do for lunch. She was still engaged in the process when Jed sauntered in and came to stand looking over her shoulder.

"Have a nice chat with Tanya?" Lacey reached for some pita bread.

"Lovely," he drawled as she placed the package of pita into his hand. "What's with the Mona bit?"

"Her real name is Mona Hawkins. Tanya Radcliffe started out as a pseudonym, but it didn't take her long to decide she preferred it to Mona, for obvious reasons. You have to admit, Tanya suits her." Lacey straightened, a wedge of sharp cheddar cheese in her hand. "If you'll warm the bread in the oven, I'll make a filling."

"I'm here to help," he mocked, moving over to the oven and arranging two rounds of pita inside. "What does she write?"

"Didn't she tell you?" Lacey began grating the cheese into a bowl and deliberately kept her tone light and unconcerned. What did it matter to her if Mona had been trying to seduce Jed? Still, there was such a thing as propriety, even in Los Angeles, and it just didn't seem right to go around seducing your neighbor's house guest! "She's made a fortune writing bodice rippers."

A glance over her shoulder showed her Jed's totally blank expression. "You know, historical romances. The sort where a beautiful young woman gets carried off and ravished by a handsome, dashing pirate who turns out to be a disinherited duke or something."

"I see." Jed lowered his lashes consideringly. "She has, I take it, an active imagination."

"Oh, no. Mona—excuse me—Tanya knows whereof she writes," Lacey retorted, unable to repress a wave of humor. "She's always getting herself carried off by the most fascinating men, oil-rich sheikhs, notorious underworld figures, obscure Hungarian counts, you name it. Men find her quite fascinating and she returns the favor. Who knows? Play your cards correctly and she might be persuaded to let herself be carried off by a rich antiestablishment type."

"Not a poor, thirty-six-year-old hippie?"

"I'm afraid not. Tanya has her standards, and she's enormously practical beneath that scatterbrained, flighty exterior. Lucky for you you're rich." Lacey added minced hot peppers to the grated cheese and a dollop of mayonnaise and some lemon juice. "I'm surprised she didn't get around to giving you the exciting facts of her life. That's usually first on her conversational agenda."

"I suppose we never got around to it," Jed told her calmly, his voice heavy with meaning, "because we spent the time discussing you."

"Me!" Lacey whirled around, the bowl of cheddar

filling in hand, and stared at him. "What do you mean, you discussed me?" She made no attempt to conceal her outrage. The thought of Jed talking about her with someone like Mona was too much. "I can't imagine either of you having any great interest in my background."

"Don't glare at me like that, I'm liable to burn the pita bread." He leaned over to remove the heated rounds, neglecting to use an implement. An instant later he flung the too-hot bread onto a nearby plate and waved slightly singed fingers in the air. "Your friend Tanya or Mona or whatever came over to borrow a cup of caviar or camembert or something. She is a little flighty, isn't she?" he observed as if only now noting the fact.

Lacey simmered in silence, fully able to imagine her neighbor breezing through the door, kimono flying, asking for a cup of caviar. Not deigning to respond to Jed's observation, she filled the pita bread with the cheese mixture, and they sat down to eat.

"At any rate," Jed plowed on between bites, "she started drawing parallels between the two of you, said you were both self-made women and I asked her what she meant." The gold and brown eyes met Lacey's hazel gaze over the edge of the stuffed pita bread. "Why didn't you tell me your father gambled away everything he owned before he died? That everything you've got—your business, your apartment—you've built from scratch?"

Lacey stilled for a long moment, frozen by the depth of the inquiring demand in his expression. Then she forced a casual tone. "You never asked. What difference does it make?"

"It gives me another tiny piece of the puzzle. What happened, Lacey?"

77

She made up her mind not to tell him a thing, and even as she came to that decision, she heard herself explaining quietly, "There's not much to tell, Jed. My parents were divorced when I was in my teens. I didn't see much of my father after that, and my mother certainly didn't see much in the way of child support or alimony! Dad was killed in a car accident on the way to Las Vegas. It was when I was going through his papers after the funeral that I realized he'd become a heavy gambler. There wasn't much left."

"So you've been on your own financially for quite a while," he remarked speculatively. "I can see why you didn't exactly approve of me. I must seem like an irresponsible, ungrateful rich man's brat who never grew up."

"What you choose to do with your life is your own business," she told him stiffly, uncomfortable beneath the rueful sympathy in his eyes.

"But the hardworking, success-oriented side of you that had to build a business from the ground up will never fully approve of someone who's content to live off his father's money, right?" he pressed.

"I'd rather not discuss it!"

"There may not be all that much difference between us," he declared philosophically, a smile playing about his mouth. "Money is money. What counts is what you do with it. And while I may admire the fact that you are earning yours the hard way, I don't approve of what you're doing with it any more than you approve of what you think I've done with what I inherited."

"I feel another lecture coming on," Lacey groaned. "Let's skip it, Jed. I know you don't find my *superficial* life-style any more commendable than I find your bohemian one. When you've finished helping me out here in L.A., you can drop me off at your father's estate and take off to rejoin your commune."

"I hate to shatter the image even a little, but I don't live in a commune," he said. "Interesting though that might be," he added thoughtfully. "If you're serious about spending a couple of weeks at my place, you'll have to tolerate me into the bargain."

"Oh, well, as I recall, it's large enough for both of us," Lacey told him heartily. "Just make sure you confine your various orgies to the wing I'm not occupying!"

He looked crushed. "You mean you won't be joining in? How disappointing."

"Would you be interested in participating in any of my Los Angeles-style orgies?" she parried with a charming smile that didn't hide the exasperation in her eyes. She didn't really believe Jed Merlin was into that sort of thing, but the least he could have done was deny it anyway!

"I don't think you've quite gotten to that stage," he said casually, "so there's no point issuing an invitation, is there?"

"You don't see me as the carefree type?" she demanded, half amused.

"I don't see you as the *orgy* type," he corrected carefully. "I think you're far more suited to belong to one individual male. Assuming one lone male could catch you and hold you long enough to teach you that. He'd have to break this nasty habit you have of maneuvering wealthy men into giving you what you want—"

"I am not maneuvering!"

"What would you call this charade you've developed for the sake of breaking off the relationship with Clayton without losing the diamond pendant? And how would you label the little game you're playing with me by holding that debt of my father's over my head? Oh, you've got a bit too much conscience and you're a bit too practical to demand the actual money from me, but that's not stopping you from using me, is it?"

"If that's the way you feel about it, why don't you walk out the door?"

He smiled, a dangerous sort of smile, one that reminded Lacey of a grinning wild thing. Or was it a laughing sorcerer? "I told you, I've always been a sucker for interesting puzzles. Now, if you've been a good girl today, I have a special treat for you."

"I can't wait," she snapped waspishly.

"You can help me pick out the right outfit for dinner this evening. I'll let you mix and match my new wardrobe to your heart's content," he offered cheerily.

"I'd rather be surprised," she muttered, getting to her feet to carry her dishes into the kitchen. "Damn it, Jed, this is not a joke!"

"I know that," he retorted laconically. "Why the hell do you think I'm putting up with the situation?"

That stopped her. She whirled, hazel eyes flaring with frustration and apprehension. But he only smiled again.

"You will give me the benefit of your artistic taste, won't you? I wouldn't want to make a fashion error on such an important occasion as our first evening together!"

Lacey shook her head a little helplessly, knowing how a rider must feel when the stallion she is riding takes the bit between his teeth. Jed Merlin was beginning to show signs of running away with her life, and she didn't have the faintest idea of how to stop him.

She was still feeling somewhat dazed that evening when she found herself being deftly shepherded about with a casual, masculine sophistication that seemed to overwhelm her. Maybe the nervousness she'd been living with for so many days was finally catching up with her, threatening to swamp her. Perhaps having someone else involved, even though he didn't know the full reality of the situation, was proving to be a weakening factor. There was a growing temptation to pour her troubles out to Jed, tell him everything, and let him give advice.

But that was ridiculous. Jed was better off not knowing the extent of the situation. Let him go on thinking she was a scheming little hussy bent on maneuvering a soon-to-be-ex boyfriend.

Why was everything becoming so confused? she wondered bleakly as she ordered half-heartedly from the expensive menu. The restaurant overlooked an exotic marina filled with luxury seacraft of all shapes and sizes. The gently rocking boats were colorfully lit, an entrancing sight at night. Inside, candlelight, polished silver, and vast quantities of greenery provided an elegantly casual, deeply romantic setting.

Lacey finally glanced up from her menu, having managed to decide on the scampi and watched her escort through narrowed eyes. Sensing her attention, Jed glanced up, his tawny eyes holding hers in a bond of unspoken meaning. Lacey felt the shiver pass along her nerve endings and saw the gentle twist of Jed's mouth as he returned his gaze to the menu.

He was right, she thought in uneasy amazement. He had evolved into a most attractive man. He was wearing a boldly elegant buttery soft suede sport coat paired with superbly tailored dark brown slacks, and polished boots. Somehow the whole effect came off exactly right. The subdued lighting gleamed from the thick, well-shaped mane of his hair, and in the shadows his eyes seemed to gleam with a persuasive excitement.

Lacey gave herself an invisible shake. What in the world was happening to her? She wasn't interested in this man, and she had problems of her own that ought to be occupying her full attention.

But Jed Merlin was turning on a subtle, pervasive charm, she realized as she went into his arms on the dance floor. And in his case the word *charm* carried the old meaning of magic.

"Isn't this pleasant?" he rumbled softly in her ear. "Neither of us is in danger of getting a stiff neck. I don't know why I haven't thought about getting a woman the right size before now."

She did fit very nicely into his arms, Lacey thought vaguely. His lean warmth seemed to beckon and bind and the rhythm of the music was designed to make the increasing intimacy seem entirely natural, almost inevitable.

"Lucky for you I wore flat shoes, hmmm?" she quipped.

"What makes you think I'd be intimidated if the inch or so difference in our height were reversed?" he teased, folding her more tightly against him. "Besides, it wouldn't be me who felt awkward in such a situation. It's women who have this thing about tall, dark, and handsome men. They like to feel small and helpless, I guess."

"Have you done a lot of study on the female psyche?" she dared laughingly.

"If that's a subtle way of asking me about the women in my life, you're out of luck. I never kiss and tell."

"So gallant!"

"Like I keep saying, the perfect male," he agreed modestly. "But to get back to the main subject, I think it would be a good idea if you kept wearing those little, flat slippers when we go out."

"Ah, hah! You *would* be intimidated!" Lacey's hazel eyes flashed with sudden glee.

"I make the suggestion for your own sake," he countered very kindly. "You already have the notion that you could hold your own against me in a physical or mental battle. If you were to put on spike heels and find yourself towering over me, you might be tempted to do something really rash."

"Such as issue an outright challenge?" Lacey smiled with impish inquiry.

"People who get overconfident sometimes make foolish mistakes," he explained carefully, a devil looking out at her from behind the tawny fire in his eyes.

"And it would be a mistake to think I could handle you?" she prodded, unable to resist his challenge. If nothing else, Jed was managing to take her mind off her troubles.

"Oh, yes, a great mistake." There was such easy assurance in his answer, Lacey felt obliged to keep pushing.

"What do you think the outcome of a wrestling match between us would be?" she asked in amusement.

"I'd have you flat on your back and begging for mercy," he stated categorically.

"And would you grant mercy?"

"No," he responded unhesitatingly. "I'd take everything you had to give, sweetheart. A little something to keep in mind for the future."

"I have nothing to worry about," she retorted blithely. "I gave you your chance to wait for me several years ago. You blew it."

# CHAPTER FIVE

From the standpoint of her plans, Lacey told herself sleepily as she hovered on the edge of consciousness in bed, the evening had not been a rousing success. She had chosen the location carefully, knowing that some of Rick's friends frequented the marina restaurant. But she'd spotted none of them there tonight. There was still the Jameson party and that little nightclub in Westwood. No need to panic. There was time and Jed appeared willing to help her even if he was finding it amusing to bait her about her life-style and her ego.

It was laughable for him to be so disapproving of the success she was finding, Lacey thought drowsily. But, then, she was equally disapproving of the way in which he was squandering his father's success. Each to his own, she told herself bracingly. He found her superficial and in search of all the wrong goals in life. She found him irresponsible and uncomfortably nonconformist. What a pair!

But just before she drifted off to sleep, Lacey had a tantalizing mental image of Jed Merlin as he was now that she'd taken him in hand. There was a certain pleasure in having recreated her Prince Charming even if he did intend to change roles with Cinderella and go home in a pumpkin when the association was over. The lure of playing Pygmalion and having one's creation come to life? Or merely the intrinsic artistic satisfaction of bringing out the most attractive features of an object? Perhaps her career was invading more aspects of her life than she realized! Lacey fell asleep with a tiny smile on her lips.

It was later, much later, when her dreams began to take on that elusive quality that makes some seem so very real. She lay snuggled in an unfamiliar, wholly satisfying warmth she longed to explore more thoroughly.

It was not a soft, cushiony warmth such as one might expect from a good pillow or a down quilt. This warmth was a strongly textured thing that made her want to knead the source the way a cat kneads a cushion. Dreamily, still half asleep, she curled into it spoon-fashion, letting it envelop her from head to toe. She sank back into sleep.

It wasn't until the drugging warmth began stroking the curve of her hip and the length of her thigh that Lacey once again struggled up into a twilight level of consciousness. Some dreams were admittedly more real than others, but she'd know Jed Merlin's touch anywhere.

Dreamily she arched beneath his hand, too content and drowsy to question his presence in her bed. The blissful stroking continued, and when she moved vaguely in response, another element was added to the growing net of sensation: languid, tender kisses brushed her cheek and burrowed beneath her hair to find her ear.

The velvety darkness of the room contributed to maintaining the safe, dreamlike quality of the seduction. Lacey knew it and at the same time knew she wasn't ready to halt it. She wasn't sure she could halt it. Jed seemed to be taking charge of the situation.

"Jed?" She stirred as he found the hem of her short filmy apricot nightgown.

"Hush, Lacey, love. I want you tonight and I think you want me. Let it happen, love. Let it happen . . ."

His words were a deep purr in her ear, as seductive as the sensitive fingertips moving with exquisite excitement up under her nightgown.

"No, I . . ."

But her protest was half-hearted, and she knew he must have sensed it at once. The truth was she didn't want him to stop touching her, caressing her. She was thrilling to the lazy, feather-light circles he was drawing on the inner softness of her thigh. Lacey wanted more of him before she called a halt to the delightful torture.

"Relax, sweetheart, and let me show you I can be the man you want—the man of your dreams. Close your eyes, Lacey, love, and come away with me."

He was hypnotizing her with that deep husky voice. Lacey couldn't find the strength of will it would take to pull herself fully awake. Her body was luxuriating in the random patterns he was outlining and finding a compelling, enchanting quality in his touch. Her mind longed to sink beneath the spell his voice created in the darkness—to sink down onto the magic carpet and let him carry her away. She longed to be taken away by him until morning would force reality back upon her.

Slowly, almost lazily, as if there were all the time in the world and he wanted to take it, Jed's palm followed the fullness of her thigh up to the contour of her waist. The apricot material of the gown flowed over his arm, a gossamer veil in the shadowy room. Lacey's lashes fluttered and then lay still as she awaited the next caress.

When it came, a trailing of his fingertips across the silky skin of her stomach, she sucked in her breath. The tingling anticipation in her was going to grow into something quite unbearable, she realized dazedly.

"I love the feel of you," he whispered throatily, burying his lips against her throat. "So soft and warm and womanly."

"Oh, Jed," she heard herself moan thickly as her knee lifted reflexively in response to the heightening passion. "I thought you liked tiny, fragile women." There was a sexy, inviting thread of humor in her words, so confident was she now of his answer.

"I didn't know what I was missing," he drawled, a heavy layer of passion coating each word. "Perhaps that's why I never found my ideal woman. I was always looking in the wrong places."

"I told you to wait for me," she pointed out.

"Are you going to spend all night saying 'I told you so'?"

"No!" She turned toward him, her fingertips coming into contact with the pelt of curling hair on his chest. With a sigh of pleasure she traced designs there, her nails scraping lightly, enticingly across the flat nipples and then tugging gently on a twist of hair.

He laughed softly as she taunted him with her fingertips and under the provocation of the deep-chested sound Lacey explored farther. When she ran her hand lightly down the sinewy length of his ribs to his waist, she realized he was wearing nothing.

And, although she should have known he would be naked since he had come so boldly to her bed, it was still a shock. With a tiny gasp she drew her hand sharply away from the taut line of his hip.

"Don't stop," he pleaded persuasively, trapping her retreating fingers and guiding them slowly back to his thigh. He felt her tremble and instantly soothed her with tiny kisses at the base of her throat. But he didn't release her hand. Instead, he urged it toward even more intimate contact.

"You feel so—so warm," she marveled.

"Not nearly as warm as you are," he rasped. His mouth trailed down to the rounded shape of her breast and he edged aside the material of her nightgown until one budding, eager nipple was exposed to the touch of his tongue.

When he caught the hardening tip softly but firmly between his teeth Lacey moaned passionately. She wanted him! She didn't pretend to comprehend the level of her own desire or how it could have taken her by storm like this, but there was no turning back now. She wanted him with a primitive desperation that seemed all the more undeniable because it was being evoked in this dreamlike atmosphere. There was no room for rational thought or for reasonable assessment of what she was doing. She was being swept away in a snare of magic spun by a master sorcerer.

"Let me take what belongs to me tonight." There was a grating, hungry demand in the velvet-dark voice as Jed lifted his head long enough to find her lips.

Lacey's head moved restlessly on the pillow, not in a gesture of refusal but in a sensual agitation. He caught her mouth with his, though, and held her still. When his tongue surged forcefully between her teeth, his probing fingers moved lower down the line of her hip.

Her body arching wildly in reaction, Lacey's stifled moan of desire was a pleading whimper in her throat. She stretched wide her fingers and clung to his muscular back, pulling him toward her with abandon.

"Yes, my lovely Lacey, yes, yes, and yes. But not quite yet, not quite yet," he growled into the depths of her mouth.

She didn't argue with him. Instead, Lacey used her body in the instinctive, persuasive manner of a woman who has come alive beneath her lover's touch.

Gently she scored the length of his thigh with her nails, and when he groaned, she continued the exciting punishment up the strong spine to the base of his neck. Her hips sought his with a wanton need that would have shocked her if she hadn't been so heavily aroused.

His bare feet trapped hers and his hair-rough legs became entangled between her own smooth ones.

"Oh, please . . . please!" Her cry was half plea, half command.

"I will, my sweet, I will." But he didn't.

Why did he hold back? She knew he was as aroused as she. Every muscle, every lean line was taut with his need. With increasing feminine aggression she began making more urgent demands. Her fingers danced an erotic, probing pattern across his shoulders, pausing to sink deeply into his flesh and then moving on to attack gently another portion of his body. Willingly she let her nightgown slide away.

Jed's breath came more thickly and she sensed his control slipping. In another few moments he would be a sorcerer driven to more dangerous forms of magic. And that was the way she wanted him, Lacey knew. With all her heart she wanted Jed Merlin swept as helplessly away on the magic carpet as she herself was.

His caresses roughened in a most exciting way, reflecting the rising level of his desire. The fingers that tormented the secret area of her pleasure between the softness of her thighs began to move more raspingly, more tauntingly. He dropped shallow little kisses into the delicate pit of her stomach and then wove a hot trail up to a point just below her breasts.

"Your scent, your taste are driving me wild," he confessed on a muttered groan as he used his teeth tenderly on her nipple. She felt his tongue emerge to wrap the taut bud, and at last Lacey knew she could stand no more.

"Jed, Jed, I want you!" She pushed at him since he would not come willingly to cover her body with his own. She pushed, using her strength to force him onto his back beside her.

She heard his sigh of passion as she flowed across him, her body molding itself to his with fierce, demanding desire. Her legs sprawled along his as she urged him into her warmth.

"I want you too, Lacey, love," he groaned, opening his arms to fold her against his chest. She rained kisses across the line of his cheek up to the edge of his hair, and then she nibbled a little violently on the lobe of his ear.

"You're all the woman I want or need tonight!" When she clung to his shoulders, sinking her teeth sharply into one thrusting muscle, his hands slid abruptly down her back to the twisting hips above his own. Then he pulled her forcefully, masterfully, sensually down onto himself.

"Oh!"

The impeded shout was half blocked by her unexpected

gasp. Lacey's body was wracked by shiver after shiver as she absorbed the erotic impact of their union. She knew from the hoarse male groan and the trembling in him that he was equally shaken.

For a long moment they lay bound together, savoring, adjusting, learning. Then, slowly at first, but with increasing power, Jed began to move beneath her, guiding her into his rhythm.

Lacey was caught up in it at once, soaring with him as they spun quickly out of control together. Her breath came rapidly between her parted lips and a sheen of perspiration dampened them both.

Desperately she clung to him, face buried alongside his head in the pillow beneath him. She felt his fingers digging passionately into the resilient flesh of her buttock and the small pain was converted by the magic of the moment into a savage pleasure.

At last the power in them both spilled over into shimmering waves of discharged electricity that fell to earth as sheet lightning, wave after wave of it descending, racing along nerve endings until it had drained everything from them.

Lacey clung to the long quiet that followed, strangely reluctant to accept the return of normalcy. With it would come the dismay, the self-disgust, the embarrassment. *Two days,* she thought as she floated toward the surface of the quiet pond. *I've only known him two days. There is no pretense of love between us. What have I done? What have I done?* She didn't even want to open her eyes and meet his.

But the inevitable came at last. Still lying in a damp sprawl along his length, Lacey felt Jed's breathing return to normal and the hands around her back began moving with an absent tenderness. She knew when she lifted her lashes she would find him waiting for her.

And he was. But the golden depths of his eyes weren't full of the triumphant satisfaction she had expected. Instead there was a warm, devilish, teasing light flaring from behind mockingly lowered eyelids.

"You're so masterful," he sighed in a fair imitation of one of Tanya Radcliffe's heroines. "I feel quite ravished!"

Lacey blinked, unprepared for the gentle humor. She flushed as she remembered the bold manner in which she had taken charge of the lovemaking at last, pushing him onto his back and compelling his response.

But the light mockery provided an answer to her current plight. She could be just as light and unconcerned, damn it! There was no need to show how affected she was by the mind-spinning emotions Jed had unleashed with his seduction. Yes, Lacey told herself, a cool, casual, superficial approach was the best one for concealing her tumultuous state of mind. Deliberately she forced a coy smile that didn't quite reach her eyes.

"I always suspected that men preferred the forceful type."

"Makes a man feel wanted," he chuckled, running his hands up and down her sides, shaping her curves. "So strong and yet so soft. How do you manage that?"

"You've been hanging around the small, fragile type too long," Lacey accused lightly, disentangling herself and sitting up on the edge of the bed. She really couldn't look at him any longer. The heat in her face was too intense, too revealing. Hastily she scrabbled for the discarded nightgown.

"Hey, where are you going?" Jed's smile gleamed at her in the darkness. "It's not morning yet. Come back to bed, sweetheart, we have a great deal to discuss."

"Such as?" she asked coolly, slipping the gown back over her head. God! Her hands were beginning to shake. Thank heaven he couldn't see the trembling.

"Such as how we're going to spend the rest of the night, for one thing," he rasped softly, sitting up behind her. He put out a hand and his fingers closed warmly over her shoulder. Lacey flinched. "What the hell?" The teasing vanished at once from his deep voice. "Lacey, what's wrong? You're shaking like a leaf!"

It was too much. She couldn't maintain the flippant façade. Her delayed shock was overwhelming her and the self-anger was too potent to be concealed or diffused with sophisticated bedroom repartee.

"Leave me alone, Jed," she grated, slipping out from under his hand and getting to her feet. She swung around to look at him, his lean nakedness a dark menace in her flower-sheeted bed. "Haven't you done enough? Sorry, if you're expecting more fun and games this evening, but you've already had all you're going to get. I'd appreciate it if you'd get out of my bed."

He lay silently for a moment, propped on one elbow, the sheet folded down to his waist. Lacey was unable to assess his mood or expression in the shadows, but she sensed a wary, considering caution in him. Was he trying to decide how to handle her? She wasn't in a frame of mind to be "handled" anymore that evening!

"What are you so upset about, honey?" he queried gently. "A few minutes ago you were an exploding bundle of passion. Do you always lose interest in a man after you've had your pleasure?" The last question was edged with the first hint of coldness.

"Do you always take advantage of your hostess?" she flung back, hands clenched at her side. "Do you always sneak up on your women when they're asleep and seduce them?"

"Lacey, listen to me. I couldn't sleep out there in your living room thinking about you. I've been wanting you all evening, talking to you, dancing with you, wondering what in hell this guy Clayton's done to make you want to dump him. I knew you were attracted to me—"

"So you thought you'd wander on into my bedroom and see what excitement you could stir up, is that it? Well, I hope you're satisfied. Because you're not going to get a chance to stir up any more, that's for certain. You can leave in the morning! I've decided I can do without your assistance. I'll solve my problems on my own!" This last came out a little wildly as Lacey refused to make herself consider the ramifications of what she was doing. She only knew she had to erect a defense against this man whom she had so foolishly hauled into her life.

"It's too late, Lacey." Jed's voice was deadly quiet. "I never get involved with anything on a halfway basis. I'm in for the duration, honey, like it or not. I wouldn't have let you shave off my beard and redo my wardrobe if I hadn't decided to commit myself to the venture."

"For someone who's so big on commitment and non-superficial relationships, you've got a lot of nerve using me for a one-night stand! Who the hell do you think you are, Jed Merlin?"

He smiled at that. "The man of your dreams, remember? Now come back to bed, Lacey."

"Not a chance!"

"Come back to bed and tell me why you're so upset," he coaxed.

"Why I'm so upset!" she echoed furiously. "Are you crazy? What woman wouldn't be upset over a situation like this?"

"A woman who was content to take her pleasures where she found them without worrying about the deeper aspects of a relationship. A woman who likes the breezy, uncommitted life-style, a woman who—"

"Oh, shut up!" she snarled. "If you're not going to get out of my bed, I'll go sleep in the living room!"

She never made it to the door. He was out of the bed and behind her, his arms sliding around her waist before she could get into the hall.

"Lacey, Lacey," he crooned soothingly in her ear. "What are you running away from? What we had tonight was something special, and you know it. Why are you so afraid?"

"Jed, you don't understand," she wailed brokenly, her determination to leave drastically undermined by the feel of his arms. She was tugged back against his hard body, cradled against the sinewy thigh and firm hip.

"Is it Clayton?" he demanded a little grimly, holding her close. "Did making love with me cause you to rethink your decision about him? Are you changing your mind about dumping him? Because it's too late for that, Lacey. You've made your choice, and I think it's time you learned to commit yourself to a decision. I don't like the idea of being a one-night stand for you any more than you seem to like the idea of playing that role for me."

"Don't try telling me you had anything more in mind

than an amusing evening in my bed when you sneaked in here, Jed," she pleaded.

"What about you?" he retorted. "What were you thinking about when you came alive in my arms a little while ago?"

"I wasn't *thinking* at all!" she hissed unhappily.

"So maybe we were both a little surprised," he chuckled. "Perhaps we both got more than we bargained for. Do you think that's possible, Lacey, love? Do you think you might have found more in my arms than you expected to find? Is that why you're so upset?"

"Jed, this is a ridiculous conversation. Let me go to bed!"

"Alone?"

"Alone!"

He hesitated. "I might be talked into doing that," he finally conceded. "But I won't be talked into leaving in the morning. Will it satisfy you if I promise not to touch you again tonight? Because that's about the best deal I'm prepared to offer at the moment."

"Jed, you have no right to push me like this," she told him stonily.

"You gave me that right. You handed it to me on a silver platter when you ordered me into your life and you cemented the contract a few minutes ago in bed. I meant what I said, honey. I think it's time you learned a few things about commitment."

"It's a cinch I'm not going to learn anything from your way of life," she protested weakly, knowing she didn't have the strength of will to go on fighting him. "Anyone who thinks in terms of a commitment based on one night in bed together obviously is in no position to give me lectures on long-range relationships! I'm not a complete fool, Jed. Don't try telling me you were after anything more than a midnight fling!"

She thought he would argue further; she could almost feel him gathering his words but all he said was, "We'll talk in the morning, Lacey. Go back to bed. I'll sleep on that damned black leather sofa. Or try to."

He released her, striding out of the dark bedroom and disappearing in the shadows of the hallway. Lacey watched him go, grateful for the concealment of the darkness. She didn't even want to see her own expression in a mirror, much less allow him to see it. The pain and uncertainty and longing would be all too clear. Slowly she walked back to the rumpled bed and sank down onto it. By morning she had to have her nerves and her chaotic senses back under control. That was all there was to it.

There was no good-morning cup of coffee carried into her room the next day, for which Lacey gave thanks. She didn't want Jed coming to gaze on her as she lay in the bed where they had made love.

Love? she demanded of herself as she stepped under the shower. They hadn't made love! How could she have used that word, even absentmindedly? Two days were hardly sufficient to develop such a complex emotion, and even if one believed in love at first sight, it hardly applied in her situation. Nor did that stupid schoolgirl crush she'd once entertained count. How could she have imagined she'd recreated the man of her dreams? Jed didn't approve of her way of living, and she could never approve of his. They had openly admitted they were not each other's type. So how had she allowed herself to be so easily seduced? Never had she been so dramatically weakened by desire and never had she been involved in a one-night stand! In spite of what Jed thought of her life, she was not the kind of woman who casually went to bed with any man who seemed attractive and interested.

No, she believed every bit as much in commitment as he claimed to believe in it. In fact, Lacey told herself grimly as she toweled dry, she took commitment a lot further than Jed Merlin was likely to take it! She sought a relationship based on love, understanding, compatibility . . .

So how had she come to find herself surrendering with such eagerness last night? Lacey's teeth came down rather violently on her lower lip in an expression of self-disgust. As if she didn't have enough problems as it was!

"Nothing like the warm, welcoming, cheerful, loving expression on a woman's face the morning after," Jed mocked softly as Lacey walked into the kitchen and found breakfast almost ready. "Makes a man feel like he must have been hell-on-wheels in bed! Here, have a cup of coffee. Maybe it will help."

"I should have known you wouldn't discreetly ignore last night," Lacey grumbled, sitting down at the white breakfast bar and eyeing him balefully.

"You want to pretend it didn't happen, is that it?" He arched an eyebrow interestedly as he poured rich-looking coffee into a white china cup. "Sorry, Lacey. I'm not about to let you forget. How do you like your eggs?"

"I'm not really very hungry."

"Fine. I'll scramble them. You can slice the grapefruit."

"Jed—" Lacey broke off. Somehow she had to get a handle on this situation! The feeling of losing control had mushroomed into downright panic, she thought, stricken.

The problem of removing herself from Rick Clayton's life was beginning to pale into insignificance compared to the one of dealing with Jed Merlin! "Jed, this has all been a mistake on my part."

"Stop waving that knife around so recklessly. I'm nervous enough as it is!"

"*You're* nervous! Why should you be nervous? You've had a few free meals and a toss in bed. What more could a man want? I'm sending you on your way with no more demands on your time!"

"It's okay, honey, I've got plenty of time. You can make all the demands you like," he growled meaningfully. "Besides, I'm stuck with this new image until the beard grows out. You might as well take advantage of your creation!"

"Won't you be serious? I'm trying to tell you I've changed my mind! I don't need your help anymore, I'll find some other way of easing out of the situation with Rick Clayton. I'm asking you to leave, Jed, before anything else happens—"

Once again Lacey was forced to break off in the middle of trying to get through to him, but this time the mechanism that called a halt to her tirade was the chiming of the doorbell.

Still holding the grapefruit knife, Lacey turned to stalk into the living room and over to the door. She flung it open to reveal her neighbor Mona, attired this morning in a sweeping concoction of lace and satin. Her red hair flowed down around her shoulders and her green eyes sparkled with delight.

"For you," she declared magnanimously, holding forth a small package and an accompanying note.

Lacey stared at her, trying to assimilate things. She was

terribly conscious of herself in jeans and a plain emerald green shirt in the face of Mona's glorious peignoir. "I don't understand, Mona. What is this?"

"How should I know, darling?" Mona glanced around the taller Lacey and saw Jed coming across the black granite floor. "Oh, you're still here? How marvelous! We really must get together again. Perhaps you and Lacey would like to come over this evening? I'm having a few friends—"

"Mona, what in the world is this all about? Why are you standing on my doorstep at this hour of the morning giving me presents?" Lacey demanded irritably, reaching out to take the proffered gift.

"But I'm not, Lacey, dear! Weren't you listening? I just now found the nicest young man standing outside your door holding these and about to knock. Naturally I said I would be happy to save him the trouble!"

"Naturally," Lacey repeated drily. "What young man, Mona?"

"A delivery person," Mona told her vaguely. "Aren't you going to open it, Lacey?"

Jed came close, standing beside Lacey and eyeing the package and note curiously. "It looks," he observed softly, "about the right size to hold a diamond pendant."

Stunned, Lacey's gaze went back to the box in her hand. The diamond pendant from Rick? Already? But that was impossible! She hadn't had an opportunity to really set her plans in motion. As far as she knew, no one had seen her with Jed last night, and Rick was out of town for the week on business anyway. How could . . .

"A diamond? Lacey, how lovely!" Mona exclaimed. "Let's see what it looks like. I can give you a rough estimate of the value without too much trouble, if you like. I've had a lot of experience with these things. Who on earth would have sent it? That handsome devil you've been seeing for the past month? Oh, sorry, Jed," she apologized brightly.

"Think nothing of it," he told her wryly. "Open the package, Lacey."

With trembling fingers Lacey lifted off the top. There was a chain inside all right, and there was a delicate prong fixture dangling from one end. A fixture that had obviously been designed to hold a small stone.

It was quite empty.

While the other two stared in astonishment at the denuded pendant, Lacey opened the small note with shaking fingers.

" 'I never pay for goods not received,' " she read. It was signed "Rick."

She lifted her eyes uncomprehendingly. It was Mona's green gaze that met hers with knowing intuition.

"Oh, I see," she drawled in open amusement. "You never went to bed with him. You've just been kissed good-bye for failure to perform!"

# CHAPTER SIX

The relief came first, a relief so overwhelming that Lacey didn't stop to analyze the expressions on Mona's or Jed's faces. With a lighthearted toss she flipped the stoneless pendant up into the air and caught it as it fell back to earth. Rick had made everything so easy for her! He'd ended the relationship first. *Must have found somebody else while on his business trip,* she mused, unaware of the satisfied little smile curving her lips.

It was as she snagged the descending necklace that the speculation in Jed's tawny eyes made her realize she wasn't acting entirely rationally for a woman who'd just missed getting a diamond.

"Win some, lose some," Lacey grinned cheerfully. "Come in for a cup of coffee, Mona or Tanya or whoever you are today? Jed makes terrific coffee."

"I'd love to, Lacey, but I really must be getting back to Justin and Elena. I left them alone in bed together and I can't wait to see what happens!"

"Voyeur," Lacey charged good-naturedly. "Don't look so shocked, Jed. Justin and Elena are two characters in her latest masterpiece. Thanks for the invitation for this evening, Mona. I'll try and stop by."

103

"The invitation," Mona pointed out carefully, "is for both of you."

"Oh, Jed probably won't be in town tonight. See you later." Lacey closed the door in her neighbor's face and turned to find Jed watching her with wry disgust.

"So I probably won't be in town tonight, huh? You are one bossy little kid, Lacey, who's turned into a downright managing sort of woman. What makes you think I'm going anywhere this afternoon except possibly to the beach?" He stood with folded arms, legs planted, and eyes hooded. Lacey didn't care for the speculation that still looked out at her from behind those thick brown lashes.

"But, Jed," she tried to say very brightly, "there's no longer any need for you to stay. I've got what I wanted and I wouldn't dream of imposing on you any longer."

"That brings up an interesting point," he drawled, dropping his arms and turning back toward the kitchen. "You didn't quite get what you wanted. There's no diamond in that pendant. Yet you're acting as if this is the best of all possible worlds. Fifteen minutes ago you were waving a grapefruit knife at me and accusing me of using you as a one-night stand. Now you're calmly dismissing me as if I were an employee for whom you no longer have any use. And what happened to the two weeks you wanted on the Merlin estate?"

Some of Lacey's euphoria died as she was forced to acknowledge that her actions were probably more than a little mystifying. She bit her lip for a brief second as she remembered Jed saying he was fond of puzzles.

"Oh, Jed, it's hard to explain. Let's just say I wanted out of that relationship with or without the diamond and Rick has made it easy for me by breaking things off before we had to get too involved in this charade."

He glanced at her over his shoulder as she automatically picked up the knife and went back to work on the grapefruit. Then he focused his attention on the eggs he was cracking into a bowl.

"Mona was right, wasn't she?"

"About what?"

"You weren't sleeping with him." There was a pleased satisfaction in his voice that only an absolute idiot could have missed, Lacey realized grimly.

"It's really none of your business, Jed," she declared coolly. Industriously she worked on the ruby red grapefruit.

"I was pretty sure you hadn't been too heavily involved with this Clayton," he went on as if she hadn't spoken. "Not after the way you gave yourself to me last night. You may have grown into a somewhat arrogant, maneuvering sort of female, but in my arms last night you were completely honest with me and with yourself. At least for a while. It gave me another little insight into the puzzle, Lacey, love, and that insight tells me you couldn't have been too emotionally entangled with Clayton. But it was nice to have it confirmed," he concluded blandly, tossing the eggs into the pan.

Lacey stared at his back, a mixture of dismay and outrage in her blazing hazel eyes. "Talk about arrogance! You of all people have just had proof that I don't need to be emotionally entangled with a man in order to go to bed with him! My God! I've only known you for two days and . . . and . . ." She broke off furiously, aware that her words

105

were cutting into herself much more deeply than they could possibly be cutting into him.

He swung around on his booted heel, leaving the eggs to their fate, and started toward her. "But you *are* emotionally involved with me, Lacey, love," he growled, reaching for her as she instinctively backed away. He caught her shoulders and pulled her close, his eyes meeting hers on almost the same level.

"No!" Dear Lord! Why did the protest have to come out sounding so weak?

"Of course you are," he murmured, his eyes softening as he took in her shocked look. "You've remade me into the man of your dreams. The man to whom you once proposed. How could you not be involved with me? And I, like it or not, am thoroughly involved with you."

Lacey blinked at the small confession, a wild weed of hope pushing its head sturdily up through the welter of her emotions. "You . . . you are?"

"Lacey, you little fool, do you think I'd shave off my beard, put on a pair of designer jeans, and tolerate the machinations of just any female? I knew ten minutes after I arrived on your doorstep I was going to be involved with you."

"But . . . but, Jed, this is ridiculous. We've grown up into two entirely different sorts of people. We have nothing in common and—"

"Why don't you just give it time, honey?" he soothed gently, running his fingers lightly up and down her arms. The tawny eyes were smiling at her, a deep, hypnotizing smile that was really another bit of sorcery. "Come home with me as you originally planned. Spend a couple of

106

weeks or a month at my place and we'll find out if we're really so very different.''

Lacey heard the temptation in his voice and found herself longing to yield to it. Last night had affected her deeply; how could she deny it? She wanted more of the magic, but did she dare risk an affair with Jed Merlin?

And an affair was all he was offering. In the short time they'd had together since he'd walked back into her life there had been no indication that Jed had changed his mind about marriage. At twenty he'd declared his intention never to marry and he certainly wasn't hinting at it now!

But why should that matter to her? After her own shallow, disappointing marriage, Lacey had come to the same conclusion. It wasn't her fault she hadn't been able to find someone with whom to share a wild, torrid affair in the two years she'd been divorced. It wasn't as if she hadn't been looking!

A faint odor of something burning drifted across the kitchen.

"Jed! The eggs!"

"Damn the eggs. Say you'll come with me, Lacey."

She felt the urgency in him. It communicated itself to her through his touch, his eyes, his whole being. He really did want her, she thought dizzily. The smell of scorched eggs grew stronger.

"I . . . I . . . Jed, there's no longer any need for me to go away," she hedged, knowing she was still searching for some reassurance. Everything was happening too fast. The sensation of losing control was plaguing her once more. "I only wanted the time at your estate so that it would look as though I'd gone off with a new flame. Now that Rick's taken the initiative . . ." *And now that I no longer need the safety of your high walls and guard dogs,* she added silently, *I don't have any real excuse for going away with you.* It occurred to Lacey that although she was grateful to be free of the vague threat she'd sensed from Rick Clayton, she was suddenly disappointed at no longer having a legitimate reason for allowing herself to go with Jed. It would have made the decision much easier.

"You don't need me to fend off another man now, Lacey. I know that. Which means that if you come away with me, it will be solely because you want to do that. Please come, Lacey."

She drew a deep breath, hovering on the brink. "Jed," she began earnestly, resting her fingertips on his shoulders. "If . . . if I came to stay with you for a couple of weeks, it would have to be on the understanding that . . . that we won't be sleeping together. We would have to agree that we would use the time to get to know each other."

"You don't think we could get to know each other fairly well in bed?" he mused, but his tone was light, filled with relief.

"I think that would make for a very limited acquaintance!"

"I see. You want the two weeks to assess my lotus-eating life-style, is that it? Going to decide whether or not you can wean me from my irresponsible ways?"

"Something like that, I suppose," she shot back, goaded. "Jed, be reasonable. There's a good chance we're entirely incompatible, and you know it!"

"Is that a major factor in an affair?" he inquired softly.

"Those eggs are burning, Jed!"

"Is it?" he persisted. "Will I have to become a wealthy

success instead of a wealthy non-success in order to hold your interest?"

"Jed! The eggs!"

"Say you'll come with me and I'll rescue the eggs, damn it!"

"All right, all right, I'll come."

"Good," he grinned, releasing her with abrupt satisfaction to rush back to the stove.

"But no sex!" Lacey added starkly.

"How are you going to resist me?" he challenged wickedly, sweeping the singed eggs out of the pan and into the sink disposal. "Pygmalion couldn't resist his own creation, remember?"

"Jed, I mean it!"

"Okay, okay, whatever you say, honey. You want to start cracking open a few more eggs while I rinse out this pan?"

He didn't believe her, Lacey thought wryly as she picked up an egg. He thought she would always surrender as easily as she had last night. Jed Merlin had a few things to learn about her, she decided grimly.

They eventually ate breakfast in an atmosphere heavily influenced by Jed's satisfaction and masculine anticipation. He made plans, issued instructions, and teased Lacey incessantly.

"What about Mona's party?" Lacey attempted valiantly at one point when he'd announced his intention of leaving for his home right after breakfast.

"Mona can invite Justin and Elena instead of us," he retorted.

"I doubt if they'll be able to come," Lacey muttered.

"Justin will probably be too busy ripping off Elena's bodice!"

"Those disinherited dukes turned sea captains always did have all the fun."

"Well, there are one or two things I should take care of down at the shop," Lacey said slowly.

"I'll go with you."

Lacey sighed. She was being swept off her feet. Why was she so ambivalent about the whole process?

An hour later Jed poked interestedly around the samples of furniture and accessories housed in the shop while Lacey made phone calls and generally tidied up loose ends in preparation for a two-week vacation. Vacation somehow sounded better than fling.

"Is this one of your designs?" he remarked at one point, bending over some of the Hadley sketches.

"Yes."

"I don't see any black-and-white drama," he murmured. "It looks like a home. A real home."

"Exactly what it's supposed to be!"

The tawny eyes warmed. "A very versatile lady, aren't you? You've put together a thriving little enterprise here. You must have inherited your father's talent for building a business."

"I seem to have also inherited his weakness for gambling," she observed, watching as he glanced again at the sketches.

"You think running off with me will be a gamble?"

"Isn't it?"

He considered the point. "Possibly. From your point of view. After all, you don't know for certain you'll be able to continue shaping me up into the perfect male. But you've made a good start, look at it that way. Have a little confidence in yourself, honey. Let's see a little of that determination you had when you were thirteen."

"Many more bracing remarks like that and I'll cancel out completely."

But by noon they were packed and on their way in the white Audi. Lacey sat back as Jed fought his way through L.A. traffic, heading toward the freeway out of town.

"We're going up the coast route?" she finally roused herself to observe.

"A much more romantic drive, don't you think?" He threw her a teasing grin.

"It will take longer to get to Carmel."

"We've got time."

Well, she decided, if he wasn't concerned when they arrived at the Merlin estate, why should she be? It was a sign of her own inner agitation, she supposed. Even with the ground rules firmly in place, Lacey was having doubts about the whole project. The feeling of being manipulated was a new one to her, and she wasn't at all certain she liked it.

But Jed was still riding a satisfied, masculine high and his conversation more than made up for Lacey's moodiness. He talked easily as he drove, coaxing her into a better frame of mind. By the time they stopped for lunch in San Luis Obispo, Lacey was finally beginning to relax. She could handle the situation, damn it! She'd always been able to handle situations. Besides, nothing was really changed. Hadn't she originally planned to spend a couple of weeks at the Carmel estate?

She was still giving herself bracing little pep talks as Jed piloted the nimble Audi past San Simeon, the site of

111

Hearst castle, and on into the rough, rocky Big Sur country. Here the narrow two-lane road twisted and snaked as it clung to the cliffs of the Santa Lucia Range. The ocean foamed and roared on the rocks below. There was little traffic in the late afternoon, and Jed took his time as dusk began to descend. It was a stretch of picturesque but potentially treacherous highway, and Lacey was glad Jed treated it respectfully. Another man, given the sportscarlike feel of the Audi, might have been tempted to test himself and the car a little.

"Damn," Jed growled, breaking off a comment on the spectacular scenery to glance in the rearview mirror. "There's one on every two-lane road."

"One what?"

"Some fool who thinks roads like this should be driven as if they were six-lane freeways," Jed grumbled.

Lacey turned slightly in her seat, but she could see nothing except the brilliant glare of headlights. "He isn't even bothering to dim the lights."

It was nearly dark now, and the Audi's sweep of light was only as good as the next sharp bend in the road.

"I'll let him by and hope we won't be picking up the pieces five miles from here when he goes over the edge." Jed slowed the car in preparation for utilizing the next small turnout.

But instead of roaring past, the large car behind them closed the small gap with alarming speed.

Jed swore again, this time with genuine steel, and accelerated rapidly out of range.

"What in the world?" Lacey, startled, glanced back again in time to see the other car surging after them.

"We've got a little trouble on our hands, Lacey, love,"

112

Jed said quietly, his whole attention on his driving as the Audi raced into the next curve. "Seat belt fastened good and tight?"

"Of course, but what's going on, Jed!"

"Close your eyes, honey. God knows I'd like to close mine!"

Lacey didn't close her eyes, but her knuckles turned white as she braced one hand against the dash. In the light of the instrument panel, Jed's harshly etched features were a mask of grim concentration as he maneuvered the little car with quick, deft skill.

They were traveling much faster than anyone had a right to on this road, Lacey realized, but the big car behind them was keeping pace. It was so close to them, in fact, that at one point there was a sharp jolt as the front fender of the pursuing vehicle caught the Audi briefly.

Lacey swallowed. "I get the feeling they don't want to just pass," she managed drily.

"Probably a couple of kids out for a little fun," Jed muttered laconically. "Boys will be boys, you know."

A short stretch of relatively straight highway loomed before them out of the gathering evening mist and suddenly the roar of the other car's engine increased in volume. They were crossing a bridge, Lacey realized, and at long last the other driver seemed to have decided to pass.

But her sigh of relief was barely begun as Jed obligingly slowed to let the other car by, when the larger vehicle swerved deliberately into the side of the Audi.

There wasn't even time to scream. Lacey had one panicked glimpse of the surging ocean far below and then Jed was twisting the obedient, but protesting, Audi into a tight, screeching half-circle. He braked violently, letting the little car's nose snap at its tormentor in passing.

It was all over in a few flashing seconds that Lacey knew she would never forget. Somehow they came to a halt in the center of the bridge. The murderous car roared angrily out of range, its prey safe, if shaken, behind it.

In the numbing silence that followed, Lacey drew several calming breaths, aware of Jed's unnatural care as he quietly nudged the abused Audi into a turnout at the far end of the bridge. There he switched off the engine and turned to face her. In the darkness of the car's cockpit she could barely see the cool assessment in the gleaming, tawny eyes.

Never had he reminded her more of a panther, she thought vaguely. She wished she could stop trembling. But she couldn't, not now, not after having caught that fleeting glimpse of the driver of the other car.

In a stomach-churning moment her whole world had been turned upside down, exposing a danger she hadn't fully believed in until that moment. Rick Clayton had tried to kill her. And he hadn't cared a bit about sending Jed Merlin over the edge of that bridge with her!

"You didn't get a glance at the license plate by any chance, did you?" Jed spoke with the calm of a man who survived near-fatal accidents for sport.

Lacey shivered. "No." Was it better to tell him the full truth or not? Was he safer not knowing anything at all? Lacey tried desperately to analyze the situation. Suddenly it became paramount to protect this man whom she'd dragged willy-nilly into the mess. She'd had no right to involve him in this! But she hadn't dreamed Rick would resort to such extreme measures either.

"That would have been too much to hope for under the circumstances," Jed was saying bleakly.

"Where did you learn to drive like that? You've got the reflexes of a cat!" It was the truth. He'd saved both their lives with his skill.

In spite of the seriousness of the situation, Jed's mouth kicked up fractionally at the corner. "I can't tell from your expression if you're filled with girlish admiration or adult shock at my heretofore undiscovered talents."

"A little of both. Don't joke about it, Jed. You know as well as I do that what you did back there took more nerve and . . . and coordinated timing than most people would be able to muster in an emergency. Did you do some auto racing or something?"

"Nothing that glamorous, I'm afraid. Now suppose you wipe that wide-eyed look of amazement off your face and tell me what the hell is going on!"

She flinched at the metallic thread in his voice. He was deadly serious, she realized, stunned. He knew she was hiding something. The wide-eyed look of amazement he had criticized a moment before grew a little wider.

"I don't understand," she temporized, vainly trying to think of a way out of the explanations. She had no right to involve this man! She should never have let him entangle himself to this extent.

Jed studied her shadow-darkened face, one long, sensitive hand draped casually over the steering wheel, his other arm stretched out along the back of the seat.

"Let's have it, Lacey. The whole story."

"Jed, I don't know what you're talking about! What makes you think I know anything about this?" she gasped.

"I must have left a rather poor impression of myself on

115

your thirteen-year-old brain, an impression I probably haven't done much to correct since we've renewed our acquaintance. Does the fact that I've always been inclined to be indulgent with you give you the notion I'm not too bright?"

"Indulgent!" she yelped, incensed at the idea. "Is that how you really feel toward me? You can damn well get out of this car and walk on into Carmel if that's the way you feel. Indulgent! Of all the—"

"Calm down, honey," he growled gently. "Take my word for it, the way I feel toward you now is entirely different from the way I felt toward you when you were a kid. But, yes, I have been indulging you for the past couple of days. Men have a bad habit of doing that around women they're trying to attract."

"Has anybody ever told you that you've grown up to be something of a male chauvinist?"

"It would appear we've both run a little wild in the intervening years," he retorted drily. "We can come back to the subject later. At the moment I think you owe me an explanation. Let's have it, Lacey," he added with deadly emphasis. "Why was it so imperative to break off the relationship with Rick Clayton, and what are we doing sitting here at the edge of the road after nearly having been killed?"

Lacey hesitated, torn between the impulse to tell him everything and share the burden of fear she'd been carrying and the equally strong impulse to protect Jed by not dragging him any further into the confusion. He didn't touch her, but across the short expanse of space she could feel his will reaching out to take hold of her. For some reason a brief recollection of one of the battles Jed had had with his father flashed into her mind. It had been fought in front of her anxious, childish eyes, and even now she could remember the way Jed had refused to back down.

"It's all right, Lacey," he told her gently as he waited for the explanation. "Whatever it is, I can handle it. Trust me, honey."

"Oh, Jed, I'm afraid . . ."

"I know you are. And you're so used to fighting your own battles, you don't know how to let someone else help you. But you aren't in this alone anymore, Lacey, love. It's not fair to keep me in the dark."

Lacey winced. He was right. "If . . . if you don't get any more involved, Jed, you won't be in any danger, I don't think."

"Do you really believe I'd let you go off on your own now?"

She knew in that moment that he intended to protect her. Lacey thought of the high-walled estate in Carmel and the power of the Merlin fortune. Perhaps if anyone was in a position to help her, it was Jed.

"I'm sorry I dragged you into this," she sighed. "I'm sorry I concocted that ridiculous scheme that turned out to be useless anyway."

"Just tell me what's going on, honey. From the beginning."

His voice was gentler now, but Lacey heard the determination behind the question. She surrendered with a strange feeling of relief.

"Rick Clayton started out as a client of mine," she began quietly. "I redid his Malibu beachfront house for him and in the process we became friendly. We . . . started dating."

117

"But not sleeping together."

"No, it never got that serious. Rick can be a lot of fun, and he knows a lot of people, but I knew from the beginning he wasn't capable of caring deeply about anyone. Still, for a couple of weeks he made a terrific escort."

"You liked the money and flash, hmmm?"

"Yes, damn it! I had a good time!" she flung back, annoyed at his supercilious air.

"Keep going," he grated.

Lacey glared at him. "Well, one evening at a party we became separated and I went out into the garden looking for him." Lacey shivered at the memory. "I heard him talking to another man, his partner in the import-export business he runs. Like an idiot, I went closer, not realizing exactly what I was overhearing until it was too late. They were talking about a shipment, Jed. A shipment of jewels —diamonds, emeralds, you name it—they were bringing in from South America concealed in some pottery and trinkets."

Jed let out a long breath. "And Clayton saw you? Knew you had overheard?"

"I . . . I didn't think so. I was almost certain they hadn't noticed me, but I guess they did, given what just happened on that bridge." Lacey's fingers twisted in her lap. "At any rate, I knew I had to break off the relationship in a hurry and I was afraid if I did it without any apparent cause Rick would be suspicious—guess that I knew something."

"So you called me in."

"I'm afraid so." Her voice trailed off apologetically. "Jed, please, I never meant for you to be in any danger."

He dismissed her words with an uncaring flick of his hand. "Why didn't you go to the police?"

"How could I? I have absolutely no proof. I couldn't give them any dates or descriptions of the shipments—nothing. And I was afraid of what Rick would do if they were unable to press charges," she confessed.

"My God, woman," he told her as if she were still a child, "I ought to turn you over my knee! Why the hell didn't you tell me all this in the first place? I've been going nuts trying to figure out your crazy actions. When that pendant arrived this morning minus the diamond, and you acted as if you'd just been handed a two-carat rock, I knew I was going to have to force an explanation out of you. But I never dreamed it was anything like this!"

"Where are we going?" she asked as he switched on the engine and guided the Audi back onto the narrow road. "Jed, I don't understand."

"That doesn't amaze me," he remarked a little rudely. "But don't worry, I'm in charge now. You'll be safe."

Slowly, as if feeling her way, Lacey sat back in the seat. Safe. Behind the walled fence and with those prowling guard dogs. It was a pleasant thought. Yes, perhaps Jed Merlin was the magician who could get her out of this mess.

"What are you going to do?" she asked after a moment.

"Take you home and make some phone calls," he said briefly, his mind clearly on something other than explaining himself fully to her.

"The police?"

"Some friends of mine," he corrected laconically.

"Friends! What sort of friends?"

"Never mind. Just tell me everything you know about Clayton. I mean everything, Lacey. Was he the one driving that car tonight?"

119

"No. I think, from the small glimpse I had, that it was his partner. The other man I overheard in the garden that night."

"Okay, start from scratch," Jed commanded.

Under his expert prompting, Lacey found herself remembering details she never would have thought important on her own. Obedient to the probing questions he asked, she told him everything she had learned during her short association with Rick Clayton.

It wasn't until they had passed Carmel and were well on their way toward Santa Cruz on the far side of Monterey Bay that Lacey realized something was wrong.

"Jed, where are we going? Your father's estate is near Carmel. I distinctly remember being able to drive a short distance into the village!"

"There are a couple of details about the Merlin estate that have changed over the years, Lacey, love," he told her with a slanting glance.

"Such as?" she demanded warily.

"Such as the fact that it was sold along with everything else when my father's business went through bankruptcy."

"What on earth are you talking about?" she snapped.

"We really have more in common than you imagined, honey," he remarked a little too evenly.

Perplexed, she stared at his profile.

"My father died stone broke. I spent the year following his death presiding over the dissolution of a paper empire. By the time the estate had paid off all outstanding debts, there wasn't a thing left."

Horrified, Lacey's eyes widened in shock. "Nothing? You're broke?"

"Well, not exactly, but I sure didn't inherit anything

more useful than my father's faithful attorney, who helped me clean up the mess," he admitted with a dry chuckle.

"But you implied I would be staying at the estate!"

"You'll be staying at my place."

"And where, precisely, is your place?" she gritted out.

"Near Santa Cruz. A little beach cottage. You'll like it, I'm sure. It's just waiting for a designer's touch."

"But why did you let me go on thinking you had your father's money behind you?" she pleaded. All her plans for safety were dissolving before her eyes.

"Sheer perversity at first," he admitted tranquilly, apparently oblivious to her rising agitation. "You were having so much righteous fun thinking of me as an irresponsible ne'er-do-well who had too much money for his own good, I didn't have the heart to disillusion you."

"But . . . but what do you *do*?"

"Contrary to your unfavorable opinion, I am an entrepreneur . . . of sorts," he drawled. "I," he stated dramatically, "am very big in tofu."

Lacey waited. When no further information was forthcoming, she repeated the word. "Tofu? Soybean curd? You produce it?"

"I'm afraid so. Produce it, package it, market it. It sells *quite* well, thank you. These crazy Californians will eat just about anything if you tell them it's good for 'em."

"Oh, my God," she muttered. "It figures. What other sort of business would an establishment dropout—who found himself without funds—get into? Tofu! I suppose you're an imposing figure in the natural foods world."

"A self-made entrepreneur, just like yourself," he retorted smoothly. "Tofu may not sound all that exciting, but I have a hunch it beats the import-export business hollow when it comes to the issue of legitimacy!"

Didn't he realize, Lacey thought frantically, didn't he see what his explanation of his circumstances really meant to both of them? If Jed no longer had the estate, he no longer had the power to protect both of them. She was back where she had started.

Somehow she had to free this man from the dangerous situation in which she'd stupidly involved him. Lacey didn't stop to question the depth of her feelings in the matter. The need to protect him was instinctive, an automatic reaction. A part of her, she acknowledged sadly, must have always secretly loved Jed Merlin. She couldn't drag the man she loved into such reckless danger.

# CHAPTER SEVEN

It was nearly midnight. Lacey stood staring out into the darkness, her eyes automatically following the sheen of moonlight on the ocean. Behind her she could hear a low rumble of conversation as Jed spoke quietly into the phone. He'd shut the door behind him and Lacey had no idea to whom he was talking or what he was saying.

Probably the police, she thought dispiritedly. What would they be able to do without proof? And she'd heard nothing very concrete that night in the garden. But her main concern now was Jed. He was choosing to involve himself further in her problems, and she didn't know how to stop him. Her magic genie refused to go meekly back into the bottle.

He'd been on that phone for the past hour, she thought restlessly, pulling her gaze away from the moonlit ocean and glancing around the front room of the beach house.

In spite of the seriousness of her thoughts, it was impossible not to view the rambling, weathered old house with a designer's eye. A huge veranda wrapped the front of Jed's home, overlooking the waters of the bay that foamed below the rocky cliffs.

There were two bedrooms, one of which Lacey had

politely but firmly earmarked as her own. Jed had made no protest, merely lifting one sunstreaked brow mockingly. A huge kitchen and a dining room that joined the living room completed the main living areas. Some of the furnishings, Lacey decided, had come from the old Merlin estate. She half-recognized the lovely oval oak table in the dining area and a couple of the lounge chairs looked as if they had come from far more formal surroundings.

Other than those pieces, the furniture was eclectic, to say the least—a hodgepodge of odds and ends that wound up being comfortable but not particularly proper to her artistic senses. As with their owner, however, everything seemed stamped with a certain, undeniable masculinity.

As that thought crossed her mind the door of Jed's bedroom opened behind her. For a moment their gazes meshed in silent examination.

"How about a midnight walk on the beach?" Jed came forward, taking a sheepskin jacket from the back of an overstuffed chair. He smiled at Lacey as if nothing in the world were wrong. As if, Lacey thought resentfully, the only plan he had in mind was to take her down to the beach and seduce her.

"Jed, who were you talking to on the phone?" She ignored his industrious scrabblings in a closet by the door.

"Some old friends. Ah! Here we go!" He emerged from the closet triumphantly, bearing an old blanket. "Get your coat, honey. Then you can take me down to the beach and seduce me in the moonlight. Doesn't that sound romantic?" He grinned at her with a wicked charm that demolished her protests before she could even put them into coherent sentences.

"I'll go down to the beach with you, but this isn't going

to be a seduction, Jed Merlin. I want to have a serious talk with you!" Lacey frowned at him severely.

"Whatever you say, honey."

He waited patiently as she found her brandy-colored suede jacket and belted it firmly around her waist. "It's going to be cold down there," she warned.

"I'll keep you warm." Jed took her arm as she walked forward and started her out the door. As they crossed the threshold, his hand moved absently across a bank of switches. No additional lights came on that Lacey could detect.

"How do we get down to the beach from here?" she asked, glancing ahead through the shadows.

"There's a path down the cliff. I'll show you. Just one thing I ought to mention, honey," he went on casually. "Don't ever leave the house alone, especially at night, okay?"

Lacey nodded silently, not knowing what to say. Lord knew she had no desire in the world to leave his home alone! But she had no right to stay there and put him in jeopardy.

"Good. Now, stop worrying. Everything's going to be fine."

"Oh, Jed. How can you say that? You saw what happened to us this evening! We could have been killed if you hadn't been such a damn good driver!"

"Relax. We're safe here, take my word for it. We're just going to sit tight until things are all tidied up and your ex-boyfriend is safely tucked away."

"Who's going to tuck him away? Jed, what's going on?"

"Can't you trust me, sweetheart?" he whispered gently, pulling her to a stop at the top of the cliff and leaning forward to drop a light kiss on her nose. "Remember how you used to call on me for help when you were a kid, and I always came through?"

"Like when?" she challenged, her hazel eyes narrowing as the light sea breeze tousled her hair. She pulled the collar of the suede jacket up around her neck.

"How about the time you and your parents came to visit and you wanted to ride that broken bicycle in the garage? You looked up at me—in those days you had to look up, being so much shorter—"

"Jed!"

"Anyhow, you looked up at me with those big eyes and begged me to fix the bicycle. And I did, didn't I?" he concluded in satisfaction.

"Oh, that," she retorted, turning away to start down the path visible at the edge of the cliff. "I could have fixed it myself, but I was trying to appeal to your male ego. I'd seen Georgina in action and decided to try copying her techniques."

"Georgina! Who the hell was Georgina?" he demanded belligerently, following her recklessly down the cliff path.

"That empty-headed blonde you were dating that summer. Don't you remember?"

"Vaguely," he admitted.

Lacey found the beach and started toward the water's edge, her sandals filling quickly with sand. A moment later Jed was beside her. "I used to wonder occasionally if you'd married her," she added quietly, looking out to sea.

"I'd made up my mind never to marry, remember? Why would I have changed it for an empty-headed blonde? Besides, now that I think about it, I distinctly recall you

126

telling me she was all wrong for me," he chuckled. With easy possession, Jed wrapped an arm around her waist as they walked.

"So you really stuck by your decision all these years?" Lacey glanced at him wonderingly. In the moonlight his aggressive nose and high cheekbones were etched in silver. She had no way of knowing that her own features were also cast in a luminous mystery. Her brown hair was lightly ruffled, framing the depths of her eyes, which had gone very dark.

"I got over the immediate bitterness I experienced when my parents were divorced," he confided, slanting her a glance, "but nothing happened after that to make me change my original decision. I've seen a lot of people take the plunge and wind up in court. Why go through all that hassle? A good relationship doesn't need a piece of paper, and a piece of paper won't make a bad relationship work."

Lacey drew a deep breath. "You're right. On that one point we agree. I had to learn my lesson the hard way though."

"What was he like, Lacey? The man you married." Jed didn't look at her as he asked the question, but there was a heavy curiosity in his voice.

"Tall, dark, and handsome," she told him flippantly, remembering her good-looking ex-husband. "Very successful, intent on living the good life and, I thought, totally compatible."

"And he wasn't?"

"Oh, he was compatible, all right. Compatible with two or three other women that I know of, one of whom he decided he loved more than he did me."

"Did you love him?" Jed asked starkly.

Lacey hesitated and then said with an honesty she hadn't admitted even to herself until that moment, "No. I don't think I did. We were a perfect couple, I thought. Everything in common. Same goals, same friends, same interests in life. It all came together in a mixture I told myself was love. Just another typical, shallow southern California marriage," she concluded wryly.

But there was no bitterness in her voice. Her marriage had been a mistake. The best thing to do with mistakes was to put them behind you and get on with life. Lacey had done exactly that.

"And that's how you learned your lesson on marriage?" Jed inquired neutrally.

"As you said, a good relationship doesn't need a piece of paper and a piece of paper won't fix a bad one."

"How many good relationships have you had since the divorce?"

"Are you asking me about the men in my life, Jed?" she taunted softly.

His arm around her waist tightened. "Not very subtle, am I?"

"No."

"Are you going to answer the question?"

Lacey shrugged. "I've dated a lot during the past couple of years."

"But you haven't fallen in love?" he hazarded to ask.

"No." *You're the only man I've ever loved*, she added silently. *But I can't tell you yet. I can't tell you until you're safe, and that may be a long time.* "What about you, Jed?"

"Isn't it obvious? I've lived the life of a celibate. A perfect philosophical monk's existence until you made wild, passionate love to me last night and awakened all my heretofore dormant desires."

Lacey giggled in the darkness, her sense of humor getting the better of her. "A sucker for the aggressive dominant-female type?"

"I'm afraid so," he sighed.

"What about the cute little Georginas you've known?"

"Oh, they don't count," Jed said airily. "Just getting in a little practice so that when Miss Right came along I wouldn't make a complete fool of myself."

"No good relationships, Jed?" she persisted, ignoring his teasing.

The humor went out of him, and for a moment she thought he wasn't going to answer. "There have been some affairs, Lacey," he finally said quietly. "Some longer than others. But there have been no love affairs. Do you understand?"

She did. "Yes."

They had turned to follow the water's edge. Gentle waves broke some distance from shore and the distinctive smell of the sea filled Lacey's senses. On the cliffs above there were a few porchlights still glowing from the widely scattered houses. They had the beach to themselves.

They walked for a while longer in silence, a sense of communion flowing between them. There were a lot of questions Lacey wanted to ask, especially about those phone calls. But for the moment she was content to enjoy the luxury of Jed's intimate presence. Soon she would have to leave, and tonight was beginning to feel like a moment stolen out of time.

The sensation of spending what might turn out to be a last night with the man she loved grew in Lacey's imagination. Tomorrow, perhaps the next day, she would have to leave. The thought was frightening and disturbing. But what else could she do? She'd dragged him into this, and she had no choice but to leave him in safety. As the incident on the bridge had proven, there was no safety for Jed as long as she was around. Perhaps someday the police could stop Rick Clayton. When she left Jed, she would go to them and tell her story. There was nothing to lose now that Clayton appeared to realize she knew too much.

The conflicting worries, her active imagination, and the intensity of her emotions toward Jed seemed to be boiling together in a cauldron that sent a fiery flow through her system. When Jed came to a halt and slowly drew her into his arms, Lacey found herself clinging to him in a strange kind of relief. She was vaguely aware that he had dropped the blanket on the ground.

The breeze off the ocean was chilly although winter had not yet arrived to give it a true bite. The warmth of Jed's embrace was welcomed by her body on several levels, from the simple one of warding off the nip in the air to the far more complex one of desire.

"Lacey, love," he breathed huskily as she wrapped her arms around his waist. He shaped her face, holding her still for his kiss and then drugging her with its heady wine. His lips moved on hers with slow, languid warmth, and Lacey moaned softly into his mouth.

He drank her sigh hungrily and then went seeking more, thrusting his tongue deeply into the vulnerable depths behind her teeth. Lacey shivered, clinging to him tightly. He sensed her response at once and strove to incite another of the telltale tremors by finding her tongue and forcing it into a duel with his own.

Jed's fingers twisted warmly in her hair and then slid down to her shoulders as the kiss deepened. Slowly he lowered his hands still farther, gliding them down the front of her jacket to the suede belt.

"Unbutton my coat," he ordered a little thickly as he loosened the tie at her waist.

Obediently Lacey began fumbling with the buttons of the sheepskin jacket. All of her vows not to allow him to seduce her again were buried beneath the painful realization that tonight might be their last until she could somehow get herself out of the mess in which she was involved. The idea of saying good-bye made nonsense out of the earlier determination not to surrender to Jed's lovemaking.

"Oh, Jed," she gasped as her jacket fell open. His fingers moved warmly inside to find the full thrust of her breasts beneath the amber blouse she wore with her jeans.

"You were such a skinny little kid," he chuckled softly as he cupped each breast. "Who would have guessed you'd grow up into this?"

"Into what?" She pressed her mouth against his neck.

"Into a woman who's got everything it takes to keep a man warm on a cold night!" He began working on the blouse fastenings, bending his head to touch her throat and then the upper curves of her breasts with heated little nibbles as he undid each button.

"Statuesque is the word you're looking for," she told him wryly.

"How about soft and cuddly? I think that fits much better. Cold?" He found the eager, erect nipples behind the lace of her bra.

"A little," she admitted, pushing back the edges of his

131

coat and sliding her arms inside. The heat of his body was a wonderful, beckoning lure and she answered it without thought.

"Just a second." Jed pulled reluctantly away, stooped, and quickly spread the thick wool blanket on the sand. When he was finished, he remained where he was, on one knee, and looked up at Lacey. Without a word he held out his hand.

Lacey drew a deep breath and let his fingers close around hers. A moment later she came down beside him. He arranged the warmth of the sheepskin coat across them both as they lay side by side and she snuggled close.

"I want you so much," he growled almost fiercely as he found the lobe of her ear with gentle teeth. His sensitive fingers moved with exquisite pleasure along her back beneath the loosened blouse.

"Yes, Jed. Yes, please . . ."

Her bra came away in his hands, disappearing out of sight in the darkness.

"Lacey, Lacey, I knew you wouldn't deny me tonight. What we have is too special." In between the words he showered urgent kisses across her bared breasts. When she cried out softly, he took one nipple into his mouth and teased it with a rasping motion that made her dig her nails into the contour of his back.

As he excited the rosy tip with his mouth, one exploring hand moved in a flat, fiery path down her stomach, found the opening of her jeans, and unfastened them.

"Oh, Jed! Jed!"

His name on her lips was a soft moan of passion as he refused to take advantage of the unzipped jeans. Instead, he lifted his hand higher again and began stroking her in

132

long rhythmic motions that made her body arch toward him as if compelled by magic bonds.

Magic. Jed's touch was sheer male magic, Lacey thought dazedly. Beneath it she curved and twisted and clung until she was breathless with her passion. She'd never known anything quite like the touch of Merlin.

"Feeling you come alive like this, knowing you respond to me with everything in you . . . God! Lacey, it drives me wild. Do you realize that?" His voice was a deep, velvety growl.

"I'm glad, Jed," she whispered simply. Her fingers curled into his hair and fluttered down to his shoulders as he moved his lips farther along the curving route of her body.

The rhythmically stroking hand was moving steadily lower now, each lingering stroke like a fire that licked along her skin.

Lacey twisted helplessly as Jed's fingers trailed down the outside of her thigh and wandered slowly back up along the inside, not all sure if she could wait an instant longer for Jed to possess her completely.

"It's the greatest aphrodisiac in the world," Jed muttered fiercely as he touched his mouth to the silky skin of her stomach.

"What?" she demanded hoarsely, losing herself in the sea of sensation he was generating.

"Knowing your partner wants you the way you seem to want me tonight!"

He was right. But then how could she resist the man of her dreams? Her thoughts broke off into a jumble of nerve-ruffling images as, without any warning, Jed's hand found its goal. She whimpered with desire, clutching at him as he slowly moved back up the length of her body.

"Still cold, darling?" he mocked lovingly as he hovered over her.

She looked up into the gleaming darkness of his eyes. Passion marked the lines of his face in the moonlight. She saw the longing in him, and the knowledge of his desire was enough to quicken her breath even more.

"Probably, but I don't seem to be able to feel it at the moment," she sighed and drew her fingertips down along the line of his chest. She put her lips to him, tenderly kissing the outline of the curling pelt.

With growing boldness she followed the tantalizing border until it disappeared beneath the waistband of his jeans. When she touched his zipper with trembling fingers, he growled husky encouragement.

"Yes, Lacey, love. Go on. Touch me, hold me . . ."

Gently he squeezed her shoulders, urging her to tug off his jeans. Lacey found herself obeying the silent command. The sheepskin jacket fell aside as she undressed him with clumsy haste and Jed reached to pull it back into place.

When she was finished, he drew her up alongside him and slowly, lingeringly, performed the same task on her. In a few moments they lay nude together, their legs thrust out into the chilly air below the edge of Jed's coat. Under their bodies the firm sand packed into shifting shapes.

"I'm telling myself I should take more time, make the moment last as long as possible," Jed groaned, his fingers digging urgently into the full curve of her buttock. His lips were probing the delicate nape of her neck. "But I don't think I can wait much longer for you tonight. Tell me you want me."

"Isn't it obvious? Or has your monklike past made it difficult for you to tell when a woman is burning for you?" she breathed shakily.

"A man likes to hear the words!"

"So does a woman."

"I want you, Lacey, love. I want to make love to you tonight and tomorrow night and the night after that. I want to protect you, keep you safe, and take you away from all the flashy Los Angeles glitter. I want to know you belong to me," he grated, each word a ragged declaration of his passion.

"Oh, Jed! Jed, I want you so much. There's never been anyone like you. You're the man of my dreams, my darling. How can I resist you?"

She heard him catch his breath, and in the next moment he was looming above her, his shoulders blocking out the stars as he settled his body along hers.

He wrapped her close, simultaneously parting her legs with his own and bending his head to take her lips. Eagerly, lovingly, Lacey locked her arms around his lean strength, pulling him down as if she would envelop him completely.

But at the last moment he held back, nuzzling her shoulders and throat while he teased her with the waiting power of his manhood. Helplessly, pleadingly, she arched her hips upward, seeking to complete the union.

But he continued to taunt her further, letting her feel the fullness of his desire in gentle little touches that drove her wild. Feverishly she clung to him, trying to wrap her legs around his thighs and force him closer. When he still

135

resisted, she tugged his head down to hers and bit a little savagely at his ear.

"Let yourself go, Lacey, love," he ordered roughly. "Explode in my arms, sweetheart. I want you to want me more than anything else on this earth!"

"Jed . . . Jed, please! Come to me, take me! I can't wait any longer . . ." Her groping fingertips found the muscled shape of his thigh and then his hip. Desperately she raked the hard flesh as she arched beneath him.

He sucked in his breath as she inflicted light exciting pain to Jed's side. Then, as if the action had driven him over the brink, he once more found her mouth with his own. This time his teeth closed on her lower lip with a thrilling roughness that made Lacey cry out in feminine demand.

The demand was met. As he gently pinned her mouth, he also pinned her body. He surged against her, taking the breath from her lungs for an instant as her whole being accepted the longed-for invasion.

This time the force and power of his lovemaking set up a shimmering pattern of magic that bound her close in his spell. With all the strength in her strong, supple body, Lacey held him close, responding to the driving rhythm that seemed intent on shattering her senses.

"My God! Lacey, Lacey, love!"

She heard the impeded growl, knew he was approaching the limit and that he was intent on taking her over the edge with him. She tightened her hold as he slid his hands down to her hips and lifted her against him.

"Oh!" Lacey gasped for breath as all the tension in the universe seemed to coalesce in her lower body, building toward an inevitable release.

He felt the beginnings of the shivering that would accompany the explosion and thrust once more with great finality. The power in him washed through her body, inundating her. Lacey cried out once as the satisfaction tore through her limbs. She was dimly aware of Jed's answering shout, and then the beach was thick with silence.

It was a long time later that the wonderfully warm body shielding Lacey's finally moved.

"Jed?"

He feathered her mouth lightly as he shifted to lie alongside her. "Now it's going to get chilly out here, Lacey, love," he whispered. "I hate to say this, but I think we'd better be getting back to the house. Doesn't crawling into a nice, warm bed sound good?"

"I was warm enough a minute ago," she complained languidly, trailing her fingertips along his arm as he sat up beside her.

"At my expense! In case you didn't notice, the coat fell off in the wanton throes of your passion, woman, leaving your gallant lover naked to the elements."

"Gallant lovers aren't supposed to notice such minor details."

He pulled the edge of the blanket over her and started pulling on his jeans. "I'll remember that next time. Come on, sweetheart, you've had your wicked way with me. It's time you took me home."

"Did I sweep you off your feet again?" She laughed softly as he pulled her up beside him. She stood barefooted in the sand, the blanket wrapped around her. Jed already had his jeans fastened and was picking up the odds and ends of their clothing.

"What chance does a country boy like me stand against the wiles of a big-city woman like you?" he asked sadly. "Lucky you're equally helpless against me or I'd be in a fine mess."

She stepped close to him, clutching the blanket around her as he finished gathering up their clothes. Together they started back along the dark beach, heading for the distant lights on the veranda of Jed's home.

"You're still operating under the theory that I'm unable to resist my own creation?" she teased, trying not to think of the fact that this was probably her last night with Jed for a long, long time. Tomorrow—she really ought to get out of his life tomorrow. She had no right putting him at risk. In the shadows her eyes filled with moisture. Her stolen moment was almost over. Just as if she were in a fairy tale, she had only until dawn with her Prince Charming.

"I figure as long as I shave every morning, you're going to be putty in my hands."

"Your ego must rank as the eighth wonder of the world," she noted as she climbed up the path ahead of him.

"And it's probably going to grow even larger," he retorted complacently. "Keep feeding it the way you did tonight and last night and you'll have only yourself to blame for its size. But I suppose that's all part of your clever plans."

"Meaning?" she scoffed.

"With your worldly ways I'm sure you were long ago aware that men are unable to resist women who make them feel like they're conquering a city full of treasure

138

every time they take them to bed," he drawled as they reached the top of the cliff.

Lacey turned her head to look at him in the yellow light from the veranda as they approached the house. "Am I your victim or are you mine?" she whispered softly.

"Who knows?" he grinned devilishly. "Who cares?"

# CHAPTER EIGHT

"The thing about tofu," Jed began in a lecturing tone the next morning, "is that it takes on the flavor of whatever it's cooked with. Watch what happens when I add it to scrambled eggs."

Lacey watched with womanly indulgence as he scooped the white soybean curd out of a small tub and added it to the eggs. It handled rather like scrambled eggs, with about the same consistency. Its bland flavor, she knew, would mesh happily with the main dish.

"*Voilà!* We have extended the egg dish *without* adding cholesterol. We have also increased the protein of the meal considerably." Jed gently stirred the mixture. "Have you ever eaten tofu?"

"Of course. I've had it in oriental restaurants and I've bought it occasionally at the supermarket. I've usually served it with rice and vegetables with a little soy sauce. I've never experimented with it as a food extender." Lacey peered at the eggs. "So this is the stuff on which the new Merlin empire will be built, hmmm?" She was trying desperately to keep the mood light, following Jed's lead. He seemed totally unconcerned with the dilemma in which she'd placed him.

"That and a few other products. We're starting to expand. The natural foods market is getting big. We've already got more standing orders than we can fill. I've been thinking about adding another production facility—"

He broke off, glancing up expectantly as a bell chimed. "Ah, that'll be Kal."

"Kal?" Lacey watched him stride over to the door and open it.

The woman who stood waiting on the other side simply stared in shock as Jed greeted her.

"Morning, Kal. How are things going?"

"Jed? Jed, is that you? What have you done to yourself?"

He stroked his bare chin with an absent gesture and grinned. "Come on in and I'll show you what's happened to me. And quit staring like that. Don't you know a Prince Charming when you see one?"

Hesitantly, the stranger stepped over the threshold, glancing toward Lacey with a curious expression. She was probably about thirty or thirty-one, Lacey thought, and she had obviously evolved along the same lines as Jed. Great quantities of slightly frizzed brown hair fell in waves to a point well below her waist. It was held back from her face with a band studded with fresh flowers. A long, sleeveless, flowing garment patterned with an Indian motif draped from neck to ankle, and she wore thongs on her feet. A strange gold bracelet clasped her upper arm. A pretty woman with great, gentle eyes and a sweetly curving mouth—Earth mother, Lacey thought uneasily. Who could fight an Earth mother? And why was she thinking in such terms, for heaven's sake!

141

"Kal, I'd like you to meet Lacey Holbrook. Lacey, this is Kali Rana Starr, my plant manager."

Lacey smiled automatically. If there was one thing Californians learned to take in stride, it was other people who marched to the beat of a different drum. She couldn't help wondering how often Jed had marched with Kali though.

"How do you do?" she managed politely.

"Fine, thank you," Kali Rana Starr replied in her soothing, gentle voice, accompanying the words with a gracious inclination of her flower-decorated head. "You are, I assume, Jed's new lady?"

"We, uh, hadn't gotten to the point of assigning honorary titles," Lacey muttered, aware that she must have sounded harsh and impolite, especially contrasted with this gentle creature.

"You assume right, Kal," Jed said, stepping hastily into the breach. The woman glowed up at him. Lacey had the feeling it was her habitual expression. "My new lady." He paused to consider the words and nodded. "Lacey, lady," he chuckled, trying out the alliteration.

Lacey threw him a sharp glance, but his smile only widened. Jed looked at Kali. "Come on in and have a glass of honeyed soy milk. We're just about to sit down to breakfast. Crew at work?"

"Yes, of course, Jed." Kali smiled serenely, as if unable to comprehend anyone not showing up on time. "I won't stay for the soy milk though. I only stopped by to see if you'd returned from your journey."

"Back from the big city safe and sound," he assured her, flipping eggs and tofu out onto a plate. "Got swept off my feet while I was there though, as you can see. I thought

142

I'd bring Lacey around the plant later this morning. Okay with you?"

"We will be happy to show her around." Kali smiled graciously at Lacey, who instantly felt mean and nasty for harboring negative thoughts toward this sweet Earth mother. "I'll be on my way, Jed. We'll look for you a little later."

"Say hello to everyone for me," Jed instructed casually as Kali let herself out the door. She nodded once and was gone.

"Best plant manager a man could have," Jed went on, serving Lacey her breakfast.

"She hardly seems like the typical managerial personality," Lacey observed drily. She poured cream into her coffee and sipped quietly.

"Are you kidding? Who's going to give her any trouble? Anyone steps out of line, she threatens them with endless bad karma. Works like a charm. Besides, the woman has an incredible head for figures. We've doubled our distribution since she took the job. She could have made a fortune in the corporate world, except that she wouldn't change her life-style as drastically as would be necessary to get her accepted by typical business types."

"A very useful person."

"She's the reason I can take off on the spur of the moment and come to the rescue of old family friends," Jed retorted smoothly. "How do you like the eggs?"

Lacey glanced down at her plate, her mind so preoccupied she hadn't tasted a thing. "They're delicious," she lied.

Even with her own impending departure heavy on her mind, Lacey found the tofu plant tour more interesting than she would have expected. To her surprise, the interior of the building located a few blocks from Jed's home gleamed with well-scrubbed stainless steel and tile. It reminded her more of a modern dairy than anything else.

"We're producing several thousand pounds of tofu a week," Kali Rana Starr informed Lacey as she guided her through the plant. "And we still can't meet the demand."

"As Jed once remarked, these crazy Californians will eat anything if if you tell them it's good for 'em." Lacey joked. The poor humor fell flat. Kali looked at her from the depths of her dark eyes and smiled kindly.

"It *is* good for them."

Lacey nodded, suitably humbled. "What are those machines?" she asked quickly, glad that Jed was occupied talking to one of the many employees with beards. The entire staff appeared to have come out of the counterculture movement, Lacey thought. Well, she'd always wondered what had happened to the ones who hadn't found a place for themselves in the hustle and bustle of the California good life.

"That's the soybean grinder," Kali explained. "And over there is the pressure cooker. When we moved from cauldrons to a pressure cooker, we increased our production considerably."

"Was that your idea?" Lacey asked intuitively.

"Well, yes, it was." Kali smiled with sweet modesty and Lacey couldn't help but smile back. How could you fight the Earth mother type?

"This is the press. The curd produced from the soybeans is pressed to the desired consistency. A drier curd makes a good sandwich filling base. A softer curd is good for puddings and mayonnaise-type products. We package

144

the curd in these little plastic tubs and then take them to the stores in refrigerated trucks."

Kali went on, obviously engrossed with her subject and Lacey listened in spite of her personal problems. By the time Jed rejoined them sometime later, she knew she had learned a great deal more about the man she loved.

"Ready to go?" he inquired cheerfully, putting a casual arm around her shoulders.

"Yes. Thank you very much, Kali. It was fascinating," Lacey said honestly.

"I'm glad you enjoyed the tour."

Lacey looked deep into the gentle eyes and relaxed. This woman was not in love with Jed. It was her own nerves that had made her so edgy this morning, she decided. Her inner tension was growing with each passing hour. Soon . . . soon she was going to have to find a way to leave. Rick Clayton might already have tracked her to Jed's home.

But the afternoon went by with no opportunity to escape quietly. And Lacey knew there was no point in simply announcing her intention to depart. Jed would have none of it. Slowly Lacey's nerves grew more and more on edge. She had to make an effort to respond to Jed's cheerful mood as he took her into nearby Santa Cruz for some shopping.

She went with him to the hardware store while he picked up some tools, and then he took her down to the picturesque mall where they wandered through shops and galleries. The boardwalk along the beach was quieter now that most of the summer tourist crowd was gone, but the attractions were still open on the weekends.

"Don't tell Kali about the cotton candy and the corn

dog," Jed begged as he handed her the unwholesome but fun lunch.

"She wouldn't approve?"

"I'm afraid not. She's on a mission to improve the eating habits of middle America. It's her life's work!"

"She's"—Lacey hesitated—"an interesting person."

"I know." Jed munched his corn dog and grinned wickedly. "Jealous?"

Lacey blinked owlishly. "You'd like that?"

"Yes and no."

"Nothing like an unequivocal answer," she protested, a small chuckle coming on her lips.

"Well, yes, because I suppose I still feel your uncertainty. Jealousy is a time-honored method of forcing a woman's hand."

"Or a man's."

"Oh, I was jealous as hell of this Clayton person and every other man you've known since you were twelve years old. I stood there looking at you when you opened the door and I thought, what an idiot I was not to have followed orders when I was twenty. I should have waited for you to grow up. Ah, well," he added philosophically, "you can't tell a young man of twenty anything anyway."

"But you're much more amenable now that you're older and wiser?"

"Definitely. As I said, I *was* jealous, but I was vastly reassured after that first night in your bed."

Lacey considered the air of satisfaction radiating from him and wasn't at all sure she liked it. "You think you can tell so much about a woman after making love to her?"

"I can tell a lot about *you*," he informed her with breezy confidence, devouring the last of his corn dog. "You're

146

one hell of an honest woman where it counts, Lacey, lady. You couldn't give yourself to me the way you do if you weren't feeling something more than physical pleasure. Los Angeles hasn't ruined you entirely."

"What a relief," she growled waspishly.

"And I'm going to save you before it gets its claws into you any farther. The minute I walked into that weird apartment of yours, I knew you needed me."

Lacey lifted her eyes heavenward, torn between frustration and laughter.

"But to get back to my unequivocal answer about whether or not I like the idea of your being jealous," he went on blandly. "On the no side, I have to say I like the idea of you trusting me to such an extent that you wouldn't be jealous. It indicates a nice depth of feeling."

"Us L.A. types aren't known for our depth of feeling!"

"Like I said, you're not quite an L.A. type. Not yet. You had enough sense to call me back into your life before things had gone too far. First we'll tidy up this little mess you've landed yourself in and then—"

"Little mess!" How could he treat his own danger so lightly? Instantly the lighthearted pleasure in the banter disappeared. All of Lacey's problems seemed to descend on her once more. A few more hours. She had to get out of his life as soon as possible, she reminded herself. She had to find someplace to hide, contact the police, and then wait and see if she would ever be free of the fear of Rick Clayton. Free to come back to Jed Merlin.

"Trust me to clean it up for you, okay, Lacey?" The tawny eyes fastened on her with an abrupt intensity that was unnerving. "I'll take care of everything."

"Jed," she began despairingly. "Rick's dangerous! You

saw that for yourself." She faced him anxiously, wondering how to make him see reason.

"Have a little faith in your man, lady!" Jed slid off the bench they had been sharing and reached down to grasp her hand. "Come on, I want to show you what a real pinball wizard can do on one of these arcade machines!"

By dinner Lacey was a nervous wreck, barely managing to conceal her precarious state behind a wall of bright chatter and even brighter smiles. In fact, she thought at one point as she moved about Jed's kitchen helping him with the meal, it was Jed who seemed to be getting edgy. Jed, who had been so easygoing all day long, was steadily growing quieter as the evening progressed. They were, she decided wryly, slowly exchanging ends of the spectrum. The brighter she got, the quieter Jed grew.

"Going to impress me with your taste in wine again tonight?" she asked.

"Every man wonders what will happen if he gets his woman tipsy," he returned. "Releases all the inhibitions, you know," he confided with a leer.

"Really?" she asked with blatant innocence, pleased to have elicited the smile even if it was decidedly teasing. He had been looking a little stern.

"With any luck I'll have you attacking me by midnight."

"And if I'm not assaulting you by then?"

"I'll have to attack you, I suppose," he sighed. But the brief moment of humor died. She saw it disappear in his eyes. "Lacey, how long did it take you to build up that interior design business?"

"A couple of years. It took me awhile to decide exactly what I wanted to do after I got out of college. I'd taken a lot of art courses, but I didn't have whatever it takes to become a painter or a sculptor. I knew that right from the beginning. Also, money was tight. I needed something that would turn a profit. I had always had an interest in architecture and interior design, and the more I investigated, the more I realized that if one established a reputation for being at the forefront of the field—"

"All of L.A. would soon be pounding a path to your door?" he concluded wisely.

"Nothing is more important down there than being on the cutting edge," she nodded with a wry twist of her mouth. "But you can hardly complain," she pointed out quickly, seeing his frown. "Tofu production is hardly your typical, middle-of-the-road route to success! How did you ever get started? And where did you meet all those people you have working for you?"

He shrugged, carrying the bowl of spinach pasta she'd handed to him over to the table. "They're good people, Lacey. Once, for a time in history, their ideals were the latest fashion in living. But the wave rolled on, I suppose, leaving them behind. Some of the people who were exploring alternatives to traditional living in the late sixties and early seventies were only experimenting. They were content to move on with the wave. But some—"

"Some had found a new way of life and didn't want to give it up?" she guessed, sitting down across from him with the salad she'd finished preparing.

He nodded. "When I realized the potential in the natural foods market, I decided I wanted people working on the project who really believed in it. These people do."

"But how did you meet them? What did you do after

149

you made the decision not to go to work in your father's business?"

"This and that," he said vaguely.

"Jed!"

"I went looking for adventure," he drawled. "What does any young man of twenty do?"

He didn't want to talk about it, Lacey realized. "And did you find it?"

"I found it. But it wasn't all I thought it would be," he told her laconically. "Eat your food, it's getting cold."

Lacey sighed and gave up the inquisition. She didn't want to spend her last evening with Jed prying information out of him that he didn't want to reveal. She wanted to end things on a gentler, softer note.

After dinner Lacey curled into the corner of an old couch and watched Jed select records for a surprisingly exotic-looking stereo system. "I should warn you, I'm not into sitar and acid rock," she told him lightly as he flipped through a stack of albums.

"When are you going to learn not to stereotype?" he chuckled. "As it happens, I'm not into that sort of music either. How does Mozart sound?"

"Sounds lovely."

"At last, something we agree on!" he muttered as he put the album on.

"You don't think we have much in common?" she teased lightly as he sank down beside her and cradled her against him.

"We will after I've permanently removed you from that Los Angeles hothouse," he told her firmly.

She went very still. "You can't turn me into the Earth-mother type, Jed."

150

"I wouldn't think of it." He smiled at her, his eyes searching her face. "But L.A. isn't good for you, honey. Look what it's done to you already—one stupid marriage, one involvement with a man who's now trying to kill you, an apartment that looks as if it were designed on the Black Sabbath, a life-style that actively avoids commitment or deep relationships . . ."

"You've learned all that about me in the short time we've known each other?" she marveled mockingly.

He paid no attention to her attempt at lightness, his hard face growing more intent. "Lacey, I want you to come and live with me."

Her stomach knotted with sudden tension. Lacey met his eyes, listened to the words, and knew beyond a shadow of a doubt that she wanted a great deal more than a live-in relationship with Jed Merlin. She wanted marriage.

Which was utterly ridiculous. Neither of them wanted marriage. So where had the idea come from? In any event, it was impossible to even consider the matter at that moment. Soon, tonight if possible, she would be leaving Jed and finding another place to hide. Marriage or any other sort of long-range commitment wasn't even on her agenda and wouldn't be for a long time to come. Perhaps never.

Lacey's fingers twisted together in her lap, but she faced him with a soft smile. "Jed, I . . . I don't know."

He quieted her, putting his fingers gently against her lips, and smiled. "I know that in this day and age a man isn't supposed to ask a woman to leave her job for him—"

"You're absolutely right."

"But our case is a little different, honey."

"Jed, let's not talk about it. Not now."

"All right," he agreed reluctantly. "But later we'll have

151

to talk about it. You know that, don't you? Do you think I can let you walk out of my life?"

"Oh, Jed!" Her eyes threatened to fill with tears because that was exactly what she was going to do, and she was beginning to realize how much they were both going to be hurt. But there was no choice. She loved him too much to stay and put him in further danger.

Wordlessly she flung her arms around his neck and kissed him with an urgency that seemed to take him by surprise. But he responded readily, drawing her closer until she lay on top of him.

"Is the assault starting already?" he teased a little thickly. He had one booted foot on the floor, the other stretched out along the couch. Lacey's blue-jeaned legs were sprawled between his own as she cupped his face in her hands and kissed him again.

"You know you love it," she muttered. "All men secretly long to be mastered."

"You know me so well," he sighed. "Take me, I'm yours."

"A pushover."

"For the right woman I'm downright easy," he admitted in a husky growl. His hands ran lingeringly up and down her sides, enjoying her shape.

"Remember how you once said that in a wrestling match you'd have me flat on my back and begging for mercy?" she murmured, nipping passionately at his lower lip and then finding his throat with her mouth.

"Little did I know I'd met my match. Here I am, flat on *my* back."

It was after midnight when Lacey stirred beside the sleeping form of the man she loved. She'd been lying awake for a long time, staring at the ceiling and trying to work up the courage to leave. She could put it off no longer.

She'd been lucky, she told herself as she slowly edged away from Jed's comforting warmth. She'd been given one more timeless moment in his arms. But the time had come to leave. If she waited until daylight, there would be no opportunity. Jed would undoubtedly stay as close as he had all day long. No, she was going to have to disappear under cover of darkness.

He moved slightly in response to her slow efforts, but he didn't waken. When at last she stood beside the bed, shivering a little in the chill, Lacey paused for a last, lingering look at his magnificently sprawled form. A lean, tanned jungle cat at rest.

Would he continue shaving after she'd gone? she found herself wondering with wry, indulgent amusement. Probably not. Shaving had been a concession he'd made only for her. And he'd probably drag out those old patched denims again too. It wouldn't matter. Every time she would think of him in the future, she knew that even his most irksome traits would be lovingly recalled. Lacey turned away from the bed, wondering how he would think of her.

There were tears in her eyes as she quietly threw her clothing into the wine leather suitcase and found the keys to the Audi. She dressed in her jeans and a warm, dark brown velour pullover. Hastily she drew the back of her hand across her eyes to wipe away the tears. She was doing the right thing, the honorable thing. She had to protect Jed.

The suitcase seemed unduly heavy and she used both

hands to carry it through the darkened living room. Her shoulderbag kept slipping, and she was terribly afraid of making noise.

But Jed hadn't awakened to demand an explanation by the time she reached the front door. Carefully she undid the bolt, reached down to haul the suitcase over the threshold, and closed the door softly behind her.

Taking a deep breath, she faced the small, straggly garden ahead of her. The waist-high picket fence and gate were the last obstacle. The gate had a tendency to squeak, she recalled.

With a sigh, Lacey hoisted the suitcase once more in both hands and started across the veranda. The place needed painting, she found herself thinking irrelevantly. And what she could have done with the inside! Visions of a charming seaside cottage done in rattan and white and here and there a touch of color flitted through her mind as she worked the heavy suitcase down the short flight of steps to the garden walk. She could have made a home for Jed. . . .

What a strange thought. She'd never been overly concerned with creating a home in the truest sense of the word. She could and did enjoy creating pleasant surroundings for her clients, exotic surroundings for herself, and she understood the psychology of a home environment. But to set about creating a real home, a nest of seclusion for herself and the man she loved, that was a whole new idea.

And one she would have to put out of her head until this mess with Rick Clayton was well and truly over, she reminded herself grimly. She reached the middle of the garden walk and started slowly toward the gate. The suitcase seemed heavier and heavier.

Probably just psychological, Lacey reflected. She didn't want to leave, and the weight of the suitcase was an inducement to slow her steps. At the garden gate she set down the suitcase and delicately tried to move the old metal latch.

As her fingers touched the gate, the garden seemed to explode in her face.

The whole world suddenly blazed into light, blinding light that struck her eyes with such intensity she literally couldn't see. Simultaneously a shrill, whining noise rasped her ears and the metal latch under her hand sent a tingling jolt through her fingers which could only be electrical in nature.

With a cry, she yanked her hand away and instantly used it to shield her eyes. Amid the startling turmoil she heard the front door open and she whirled to face blindly in that direction.

Jed's voice came to her from the other side of the blinding light as the rasping, whining noise abruptly cut off.

"Going somewhere, Lacey?"

The coldly laconic tone was new and chilling. Lacey froze in the blaze of the garden, blinking furiously to adjust her eyes. She felt completely disoriented and stunned.

"Jed! What . . . what in the world is going on? All this noise and light? And the fence . . ." Helplessly she stared into the floodlights, searching for his shadowy figure on the veranda.

"I told you not to go out alone at night." She heard him move and the brilliant light went out, leaving her in streaked darkness as her eyes once more tried to readjust. She stood tense, trapped in her momentary blindness, and listened to him pad almost silently down the steps and along the path toward her.

"Jed, please! What is all this? I . . . *Jed* !"

His name was a stifled yelp of alarm as she felt his arms slide behind her back and under her thighs. An instant later she was being swung off her feet and held fiercely against his chest.

"What made you run, Lacey?" he growled, striding up the walk toward the veranda. "The fear of commitment? The bit about asking you to leave your job? Whatever it was, lady, you're going to have to face it, because I'm not letting you walk out of my life this easily."

She heard the rough determination in him and a shaft of fear coursed down her spine.

"Please! Listen to me, Jed. You don't understand!"

"I understand all right," he spat out tightly. "You've been running free in L.A. too long, but tonight that all comes to an end. Tonight I'm going to teach you that you can't casually pull me into your life, use me, and then drop me when things start getting too serious."

"Jed!"

"Tonight, Lacey, lady, you're going to find out what commitment really means. You belong to me because you've given yourself to me. I'm not going to let you play fast and loose with me just because you haven't got the nerve to face the reality of what you've done."

"Damn it! Will you listen to me?"

"No! I don't want to hear all your excuses for running. I wouldn't buy any of them anyway! You're my woman, Lacey, and I've just caught you trying to sneak off into the night. If you think you're going to get away with that, you're out of your mind! I'm going to show you exactly what it means to belong to me, Lacey Holbrook. Tonight you're going to take the last fall in this wrestling match of ours!"

# CHAPTER NINE

Lacey was still struggling for breath and words as Jed carried her effortlessly up the steps and into the house. He thought she was running away from him, away from what they had found together. Somehow she had to calm him down and make him listen to reason.

But her sleek, magic panther was beyond reason at the moment. All her feminine instincts throbbed warily as they absorbed the impact of his fury. And he was furious.

The only other time she had seen Jed Merlin in a rage, Lacey realized, was when she was a young girl and had witnessed some of his battles with his father. But this anger was different, far different from that of a rebellious young man who is refusing to conform to the family mold. This was the more primitive reaction of a possessive male who has found his mate fleeing in the darkness.

He'd come after her with only one goal in mind—to carry her back to bed as if he had every right in the world. The surge of sheer masculine dominance took her by surprise but then, Lacey thought a little hysterically, Jed had a habit of doing that. Her magician crossed boundaries and flitted in and out of prescribed niches as if he weren't even aware they existed.

"Jed, please listen to me," she begged as he carried her across the living room and toward the dark hallway. Her eyes were slowly returning to normal now, and she could begin to make out the shapes of the structure around her. She didn't need eyes to tell her that Jed was naked from the waist up. Apparently he'd taken time to throw on his jeans, but that was all. Her fingers fluttered helplessly around his shoulders and she looked up into his face, trying to discern the hard angles of his features. "I wasn't running away. Not exactly . . ."

"The suitcase was empty, I suppose? And the keys aren't the ones to the Audi? Don't lie to me on top of everything else, Lacey! Even as a kid you were never very good at lying."

"I'm not lying! Damn it, Jed, you're . . . you're scaring me!" she protested, her fingers on his shoulder curling into a frustrated little fist.

"Maybe that's what it's going to take for a while. If I have to keep you on the leash with a little healthy fear, that's what I'll use."

He sounded so coolly confident, as if he really had that option open to him, that Lacey's rattled senses began to coalesce into outrage. She was willing to explain things to Jed on a rational level, but she certainly didn't intend to put up with this high-handed treatment.

"Stop talking as if you have some sort of right to man-handle me," she hissed as he moved through the open bedroom door and over to the rumpled bed. "I was trying to do what's best for both of us!"

"Were you, Lacey? Or were you just thinking of your-self?" He let her tumble to the middle of the tousled sheets and then leaned over her, his fists planted on either side

159

of her body. The tawny eyes gleamed down at her, fully visible now in the moonlight—a panther with his prey trapped between his paws.

"I can't stay here with you, Jed. Can't you see that?" she wailed helplessly.

"You're going to stay here, Lacey. You're going to learn to handle the commitment you made to me if I have to lock you up and throw away the key!"

Lacey unconsciously touched the tip of her tongue to her lower lip, drew a shaky breath, and tried to explain everything in one quick rush.

But there was no time to get the first in what probably would have been a stream of incoherent words out of her mouth. Jed came down on top of her with the full impact of his weight.

For an astonishing instant, Lacey felt the breath go out of her. He seemed much heavier than she had ever realized! Her eyes widened as he caught her wrists and pinned them on either side of her head. The full significance of the ease with which he'd picked her up and carried her into the house hit her. What had ever given her the idea that in an outright struggle she could hold her own against him?

The knowledge heightened her outrage. She was not about to be pushed around by the man she had been doing her best to protect!

"Are you going to fight me, Lacey?" he asked softly, his face so close to hers she could see the lambent flames of anger and desire in his eyes. "Go ahead. Be my guest. I warned you what would happen if you did."

Lacey lost her temper altogether. Gone in a flash was the desire to try and explain her motives. Her outrage simmered to the surface and spilled over in an angry wave of frustration.

"Who the hell do you think you are, Jed Merlin?"

"Your lover, your man, the one who has exclusive rights to every inch of you because you gave me those rights. Any other questions?"

"Quite a few!"

Without telegraphing her intent, Lacey twisted suddenly, violently beneath him. She couldn't fully believe that she didn't have the physical power to dislodge him if she really tried.

He didn't argue with her. He simply held her, letting her writhe in his grasp until she was breathless. The cool display of physical superiority enraged her and she struggled all the harder.

"Get off me! You're not going to treat me like this!"

She twisted her legs, trying to use her knee as a wedge against the vulnerable lower half of his body. But somehow he only seemed to sink more deeply against her. By the time she'd freed her limbs, it was to find his jeaned thighs lying heavily between her own.

"Remember in the morning that you asked for everything you're getting tonight," he told her savagely. He unlocked one wrist to shove his hand roughly beneath her velour top. He found the unconfined breasts at the same moment that her nails found his unprotected shoulder.

They both gasped in unison, Jed reacting to the pain she was inflicting and Lacey to the intimate capture. Neither ceased the torment.

"Go ahead and hurt me all you want, Lacey, lady," he breathed huskily as he stroked his palm across her breast. "You won't frighten me off and you won't escape."

"Listen to me, you thick-headed, arrogant bastard! I was only doing what I had to do!" she yelped, raking her hand up his shoulders to tangle it in the tawny mane of his hair. Grasping a handful, she tugged just enough to cause pain.

"Tonight you'll do what I tell you to do!" he muttered.

Jed jerked upward, wrenching the velour top over her head and freeing himself of her grip on his hair. When he came back down on her this time, he crushed the full softness of her breasts under his chest. She was suddenly vividly aware of the wiry cloud of hair teasing her nipples, and her whole body began to react to his intense demand.

The next thing Lacey knew, both her wrists were caught in one of his hands and with the other he held her face still for a bruising kiss that commanded obedience. His tongue surged between her lips, claiming the warmth beyond as if by right, and he moved his mouth on hers in a slow, darkly sensuous contact.

As an act of mastery, it was shockingly, overwhelmingly effective. Lacey was feeling stunned as he drew his hand down her length, his lips still holding hers. His bare feet shifted, trapping her ankles, and her imprisonment was complete.

When she finally stopped struggling, Jed lifted his head a fraction. The gold and brown eyes locked with hers as she lay panting beneath him.

"If you're trying to prove you're stronger than I am, you can relax," Lacey managed scathingly. "You've made your point!"

"Have I? Then we can be getting on with the next lesson, can't we?"

"Don't threaten me, Jed!"

"I'm not going to threaten you," he growled, "I'm going to wipe out the damage L.A. has done to you. I'm going to make you accept the fact that you've started a relationship with me that can't be terminated just because it wasn't staying safely shallow. I'm going to make you admit that you love me and you're going to abide by the responsibilities of that love!"

"Love you!"

"Don't look as if you've never heard the word! Or do you really need to be told what it means?" he rasped.

"Jed, I—"

"It means to care about someone else enough to take a few risks. It means to trust. It means to be totally and completely faithful because you can't imagine being otherwise. It means to—"

"Stop lecturing me! I know what the word means! Why the hell do you think I was trying to sneak out of here tonight?" she raged at him.

"Because you've grown into a shallow, superficial woman who didn't realize that when she gave herself to me it was for keeps, not for the night!" he raged back. "You got scared tonight, didn't you? You realized I was going to take you away from all the fun and games in L.A. and you panicked. I saw it coming on all day long!"

"What are you talking about?"

"Do you think you had me fooled with that bright façade? I knew you were getting nervous; starting to think about the ramifications of what you were doing. So you made love with me one last time and then tried to walk out the door. Well, it's too bad you're scared, Lacey, because you're committed. There's no turning back now. I won't let you!"

She sucked in her breath, wanting to rail at him for the way he was treating her, but the pain that flickered behind the anger in those tawny eyes stopped her tirade before it began. My God! She'd hurt him, really hurt him. The knowledge was more tormenting than anything he could have done to her.

"Oh, Jed, you fool!" she whispered in a soft, agonized voice. "I'm not afraid of what I feel for you. I'm afraid of getting you hurt or killed! Can't you get that through your head? I'm not going to stick around here and risk bringing Rick Clayton down on your neck! I love you far too much to do that!"

He went very still, not releasing his hold on her but not hurting her. She saw the flash of hope in his eyes, felt the tension in his body as he covered her so heavily.

"Didn't you realize why I was trying to leave tonight?" she went on gently, the hazel gaze luminous in the moonlight. "Jed, when this is all over I'll come back, I swear it. If you still want me, I'll come back. But for now I have to go. I can't put you in any more danger."

"Forget that part," he interrupted brusquely. "Tell me again that you love me."

"I started loving you the moment you walked through my doorway. I kept trying to stuff you into the proper category and you wouldn't fit. I labeled you irresponsible and you confounded that by insisting on paying off a debt that wasn't even your own. I thought you must have grown soft and indolent with your lotus-eating life-style and then every time I looked at you I saw a panther—"

"A panther!" But there was warm delight in the tawny eyes as he watched her eagerly, listening to her confession as if he couldn't hear it often enough.

"Yes, a panther. Hard, lean, tough. It didn't fit the image of an aging free spirit, to say the least. You kept talking about commitment and I couldn't reconcile that with a life-style that preached open and free love. Then I find out you hadn't sat back and lived off your father's money all these years. You've built your own business from scratch, just as I had to do. You're a difficult man to pigeonhole, Jed Merlin!" She freed her hands to spread her fingers lovingly along the sides of his face. "A magic man who won't stay put in the various roles I try to assign. And every time you turn around, I love you a little more."

"Lacey, Lacey, my sweet love . . ." With a strange, gentling motion Jed stroked his thumbs along her temples, gazing down at her with a loving passion that made moisture rise into her eyes. "I fell for you completely the moment you opened the door and invited me into that awful living room of yours! My first thought was that I was going to have to get you away from Los Angeles. I could see traces of the woman that thirteen-year-old kid should have grown up to be and I wanted to wipe out your past completely and let the real you come through."

"How romantic," Lacey smiled tremulously, daring to relax and let some of the humor surface. "We both took one look at each other and decided to change the other person into what we wanted!"

"Ummm," he agreed, responding a little to her silent laughter. "But in the end it turns out neither of us was really that far off base, after all! You are, under that aggressive, hustling Los Angeles façade, a hard-working businesswoman. And I knew the moment I came to your bed that you hadn't been flitting through a string of meaningless affairs. The woman I held in my arms gave herself to me completely. You hold back nothing when you make love to me, Lacey, lady. A superficial, shallow person wouldn't allow herself to be that vulnerable in bed."

"Oh, Jed."

"But when I realized tonight that you were running away, I thought I'd misjudged you completely," Jed went on with a trace of grimness, the edge of his mouth hardening perceptibly. "Lacey, how could you do that to me? Don't you know what it did to me to wake up and find you gone?"

"I'm sorry, Jed," she whispered achingly. "But I had to leave to protect you. Don't you see? When I realized that Rick must know for certain I had overheard too much that night in the garden, I thought it would be all right to stay with you. I thought we'd both be safe behind the walls of the old Merlin estate. I remembered your father's hired guards and the dogs. But when we got here, I knew you were in as much danger as I was and I couldn't jeopardize your life."

"Lacey, you're an idiot," he told her fondly. "You're as safe here as you would have been at the Carmel place, perhaps safer. And so am I, for that matter! Look how far you got tonight. And if you'd been trying to enter the house, it would have been the same story."

"What did happen out there?" She frowned, remembering her blindness and the disconcerting siren. "I thought World War Three had started in your garden!"

"It's like that all the way around the house. I set the traps every evening. During the daytime there's no real danger, because a strange car in the vicinity would soon make itself known. But at night I simply hit those switches beside the front door and we're surrounded by a circle of booby traps."

"My God! Why, Jed? I'm not complaining, but what on earth led you to take such extreme steps to protect this place?" She stared at him, uncertain.

"It's a long story, Lacey," he murmured. "I give you my word I'll tell you in the morning. But right now I need to reassure myself that you're here in my bed and that you won't try to run away again. Please, sweetheart?"

She wanted the answers, but she wanted to soothe the remains of his pain. Of the two desires, the latter seemed more critical at that moment.

"Oh, my darling," she breathed, running her fingertips gently in his hair. "I should leave in order to protect you. I ought to call the police and see if they can do anything and then find a place to hide."

"No, Lacey! You're not going anywhere without me! Trust me, honey. I'll take care of you. Please, trust me!"

She shook her head wonderingly. "I'll stay. I'm not at all sure I could work up the courage to try leaving you again anyway. I love you so much—"

He cut off her words, his mouth fastening onto hers with a fierce urgency that effectively silenced any further protest. Lacey surrendered to it, knowing the deep need to reassure him of her love.

His lovemaking held a new element this time. Lacey was deeply aware of the unrestrained hint of mastery and an urgent male need to elicit a full response from her. Something very fundamental in Jed needed to imprint itself on her as if to make certain she would never again run from him.

Lacey didn't try to fight it. She recognized the primitive

nature of the masculine emotion and reacted to it, yielding fully to the need. Tonight Jed was intent on making her completely aware of his claim and she was content to give him the satisfaction of her surrender. More than anything else in the world, Lacey wanted to reassure him of the hold he had on her.

His hands moved on her with possession and a sort of arrogance. But it was an arrogance born of a need to dominate her long enough to make certain of her, and Lacey didn't try to resist.

"Lacey, don't ever leave me again," he rasped, still sprawled heavily on top of her. His palms cupped her face as he rained passionate kisses from the edge of her chin to the tip of her nose. When his tongue surged aggressively into her mouth, she retreated under the impact, only to have him pursue and corner her own tongue.

Slowly, with rising heat, she let herself be drawn forth in a fierce love battle. It was a battle in which Jed was always the master, sometimes teasing, sometimes fierce, but always in control.

Satisfied with the victory over her mouth, he left her breathless and aroused to seek a fiery path down the length of her throat to the hollow where a telltale pulse beat rapidly. She arched her neck as he kissed the vulnerable region, and he seemed to revel in the abandoned way she was responding.

His hands shaped the fullness of her breasts, thumbs stroking the nipples into complete, throbbing arousal until Lacey thought she would go wild.

"Jed! Oh, Jed!"

He caught first one then the other tender peak between his teeth, inflicting a small violence that thrilled her beyond measure. Lacey's fingers bit deeply into the taut cords of his neck and shoulders. Then he was moving lower, trailing hot, damp caresses across her stomach and still lower.

Lacey moaned, her passion escalating rapidly out of control. She twisted and arched beneath his assault, begging with her body for the culminating act.

Still he denied her, intent on demonstrating his sorcery. His lips feathered the inside of her thigh and his nails raked gently from her ankle to the burning heart of her desire.

"Do you want me, Lacey?" he growled.

"Please, Jed. Make love to me, I need you so!"

She trembled again as he held back, inciting a level of response she would not have believed possible. She became a wild thing in his arms, struggling desperately to assume control in order to find fulfillment.

With a gasp she sought unsuccessfully to reverse their positions. She knew he wanted her, knew the heat and strength of his own passion. He was only teasing her so unmercifully because he was trying to punish her a little for her attempt to leave.

Wildly, Lacey pushed at his shoulders and was left stunned and breathless when he refused to be manipulated into a position that would allow her full control.

"Not tonight, Lacey, lady," he grated, using his wiry strength to hold her easily beneath him. "Tonight you learn there are limits. Sometimes a man has to assert himself. As strong as you are, my love, in some ways I'm still stronger!"

"Please, darling," she whispered invitingly, changing her tactics at once, "I only want to love you. Let me!"

He chuckled deeply. "Tonight I like having you all helpless and soft and yielding in my arms. You've roused the beast in me, sweetheart, and he won't rest until he's won completely."

"Jed, don't tease me like this!"

"I'm not teasing you. Pay attention, love. Tonight, I'm taming you!"

It was incredible. Thrilling, exciting, unnerving, and at times even a little frightening. Lacey wasn't at all certain that in the morning she would like the thought of having been tamed. But tonight there was a primeval element in the love battle that could not be denied. It aroused her, infuriated her, left her gasping for breath. But above all it left her in no doubt about who was in charge that night in Jed's bedroom.

Nothing she did could break his pace or short-circuit his intentions. He mastered her body with complete awareness and unalterable drive. Again and again he kissed her, sometimes playfully, sometimes urgently, and sometimes with an intimacy that stunned her senses.

In the end she could only respond and plead and struggle futilely to force the ultimate result.

At last he seemed content with the demonstration of masculine power. His hands slid under her buttocks, and he buried his lips against her arching throat. When he surged against her, taking her completely, Lacey cried out in wonder, gratitude, and love.

Flinging her arms around his neck, she clung to him, surrendering willingly now to the rhythm he established. She wrapped him close as he drove urgently to satisfy them both. The loving roughness was stimulating beyond anything Lacey could have described. Helplessly she gave herself up to the overwhelming ecstasy, succumbing to the throbbing, shimmering release with a soft, muted sound that Jed drank from her lips.

When he felt her moment of tension and the violent shivering that followed, Jed finally allowed himself to fall victim to the trap he had set.

"Oh, God! Lacey! Lacey!"

And then there was only an incoherent groan as his passion swamped them both.

After that the silence fell heavy and warm around them and the languor stole over the rumpled bed with catlike stealth. Lacey slowly came back to her senses, lifting drowsy lashes to find Jed's tawny gaze on her love-softened face. He still lay on top of her, his body entwined intimately with hers.

"You never told me," she murmured, "that you were the masterful type too."

"You know you have the power to make me into anything you like," he reminded her with a soft, lazy laugh. "I'm your creation. The man of your dreams."

"Don't you dare blame this last spectacle on me!"

"You mean you weren't asking for a display of masculine possessiveness when you tried sneaking off tonight?" He looked innocently amazed.

"I most certainly was not! Not even subconsciously," she accused with mocking outrage. "You used the whole thing as an excuse to prove that just because we're practically the same height, that doesn't mean we're equally strong. But you'll get yours, Jed Merlin."

"I can't wait," he agreed complacently, a slow, wicked grin slashing across his face. White teeth gleamed in the darkness and the tawny eyes glittered with gold.

"I know you can't," she retorted demurely. "You're a sucker for dynamic, aggressive women. I figure tonight was just an aberration. It won't be long before you're back in the palm of my hand."

"And you're back to playing Pygmalion?"

"Exactly."

"I suppose it wouldn't be very gentlemanly of me to point out that a few minutes ago you were in the palm of *my* hand?" he mused.

"It certainly would not!"

"I thought not. But for a while there, lady, you were even more of a fool for the masterful type than I am! So much for the liberated, L.A. style of female."

"Think what you like," she purred unconcernedly. "Somehow I don't feel like arguing at the moment."

He laughed happily. "Neither do I."

It wasn't until the next morning that Lacey got an explanation of the exploding garden and a few other mysteries. The story came in cool, laconic sentences from Jed as he sipped his coffee across the breakfast table from her.

"Do you remember I told you once that after I refused to go into business with Dad I went looking for adventure?"

"I remember," Lacey said quietly, buttering her toast.

"I took a couple of thousand dollars out of my bank account and went off to see the world," he went on drily. "The money ran out somewhere in Southeast Asia, and I wound up looking for work."

"You found it?" Lacey eyed him curiously.

"I found it. Or perhaps it would be more accurate to say it found me. I managed to land a job in one of the port cities unloading freighters. I was thinking of shipping out on one, when I was approached by a man from the United States embassy in that country. He . . . asked me to do him a favor."

"What sort of favor?" Toast forgotten, Lacey stared at Jed.

"Nothing much. All I had to do was take the freighter job and keep an eye open for . . ." Again he hesitated. "A couple of things."

"Smuggling?"

"Yes. Normally the embassy personnel wouldn't have gotten worried over a bit of smuggling in that part of the world. It's a way of life. But in this case it involved weapons that, according to the embassy guy, were being brought in to be used in a manner the United States government didn't fully approve. A coup was being planned apparently."

"And you located the weapons?"

"Let's just say that somehow I got involved," he told her briskly. "At any rate, one thing led to another and the operation was halted in time. The man I was in contact with at the embassy was—grateful. Said if I ever needed a return favor, I should feel free to get in touch."

"So you did. When you needed the favor for my sake," Lacey concluded gently.

He nodded, taking another sip of coffee.

"What did you do after that business with the smuggling though?" she pressed urgently.

"I kept the job on the freighter for a while. It gave me a chance to see the world. A little more of it and the evil in it than I really wanted to see, I think," he added quietly. "I got sick of the squalor and hopelessness and underlying violence that seemed to be in every port in that part of the

173

world. But I learned a few things about protecting myself in the process," he went on philosophically, "hence the wired garden around this place. Eventually I'd had more than enough of adventure. I came home."

"Just in time to find your father gone and his business in turmoil?" Lacey's heart ached in understanding. She knew then and there she would never ask him what he had seen in that far-off corner of the earth. Not unless he wanted to talk about it someday.

"Getting the business liquidated and the creditors paid off did take my mind off my previous job experiences," Jed smiled. "But by the time I'd taken care of that, I really was in bad shape. I wanted to go somewhere and hole up for a while. I was tired. Job burnout, maybe. In any event, I wanted a chance to get myself together again and start over."

"And you found these people? The ones who are working for you now?" Lacey guessed at once.

"They didn't ask any questions or make any judgments, just took me in and let me recover at my own rate. I owe them a lot. But their way of living wasn't what I needed for the long haul. It was merely a time of resting and recuperating. I'd worked twenty-hour days clearing up the mess my father had left. Eventually, however, I felt like getting back into the real world. I looked around like any good entrepreneur and found a need begging to be filled."

"Crazy Californians who will eat anything that's good for them?"

"It all fell into place very nicely," Jed grinned, his eyes lighting. "I seem to have inherited some of my father's ability to get a business off the ground. Just as you appear to have inherited something like that from your father."

"Let's hope we didn't also inherit their inability to keep the empires intact!"

"I'm not worried about it," he shrugged. "One thing I've learned is not to be overly concerned about the future. A certain amount of flexibility is a great asset in life. That's about the end of my tale, I suppose. Except, of course, for the fact that one fine day I got a call from my father's old lawyer informing me there was one last debt to be paid . . ."

"Jed."

"You'll be safe here, Lacey."

"It's *your* safety I'm concerned about!"

"I can take care of both of us, honey. In any event, we won't have long to worry about Rick Clayton and company," he added with calm assurance.

She looked at him and saw the confidence in his eyes. "Really?"

"Really."

"Merlin the Sorcerer?"

"Merlin the Practical Strategist with a Friend in the Right Place," he corrected mildly.

The authorities picked up Rick Clayton and his partner three days later. In the end it was almost anticlimactic, Lacey decided. There was a phone call one evening for Jed that he took with calm thanks, as if he had never expected anything except a good result from the forces he had quietly set in motion.

"Thanks, Aaron," he said, before replacing the phone. "No, no, that's fine. Glad to be of help. Take care of yourself, friend. I know. The feeling is mutual. If I can ever do you a favor . . ."

Lacey waited tensely as Jed said his good-byes to the

mysterious Aaron. She sat curled on the couch, staring into the fire on the hearth. Jed came back across the room and sank down beside her, pulling her close.

"It's all over, honey. Clayton and his pal were picked up by the Mexican authorities trying to cross the border this morning. Apparently they were foolish enough to try bringing the shipment on through. Probably hoped they'd scared you sufficiently so that you'd keep your mouth shut until they could make the big score. Greedy."

Lacey shivered. "And they're in custody?"

"In a Mexican jail. It will be a long time, if ever, before anyone ever hears from either of them again. The Mexican judicial system doesn't go in for all the fancy stuff about the criminal's rights!"

She looked at him searchingly. "And just like that we're safe?"

He smiled gently. "Just like that. Having that bit of trouble out of the way means we can get back to more important things, doesn't it?"

She knew what he meant. Since the night he'd caught her in the garden, neither of them had brought up the subject of what would happen once Clayton had been disposed of. Lacey felt a small chill as she considered the future.

"What is it, Lacey?" Jed asked softly, his gaze intent.

"I have to go back to Los Angeles, Jed." She spoke in a low, stark tone.

"No!" The single negative was equally low but rang with a harshness that made her wince.

"Jed, this is all happening too fast. I have to go back for a while. I have to put my life in order again and—and think about what I'm doing! Please try to understand. I need a little time, darling—"

"I'll come with you."

She shook her head, her eyes softening. "It's not necessary. I'll be back, Jed. Believe me."

"How long?" he grated.

"Not long. I promise. Do you think I could stay away from you very long?" she asked whimsically.

He hesitated, clearly torn, and she put up a hand to touch the side of his firm, tanned cheek. "I'll be back," she repeated. "But there are things that must be taken care of first. Surely you can understand that?"

He closed his eyes and exhaled in a long sigh, crushing her close. "Lacey, lady, you'll have to hurry back to me. I'll go out of my head wondering if you're getting swept up again in your old life!"

"There's nothing back in L.A. quite like the man I created," she told him tenderly. "How could I resist coming back to you?"

# CHAPTER TEN

Three weeks after Lacey returned to Los Angeles, she attended yet another party in Mona Hawkins's apartment. The stereo was fighting a losing battle with the hubbub of clever, witty conversation, and the front door had been left open because no one could hear the polite knocking of various latecomers.

Mona was fully into her Tanya role, darting about her collection of colorful, amusing people as if she were a butterfly going from one exotic flower to the next. The full skirt of a daring scarlet evening gown trailed behind her as she circulated through the crowd. The party had been catered by one of the most exclusive agencies in the area, and no expense had been spared at the bar.

Lacey, sipping at a potent Margarita, watched her beautiful hostess and smiled secretly to herself as Mona swept toward her.

"Are you having a good time, dear? But of course you are! What other sort of time could someone have at one of my parties! Listen, Lacey, do you see that divine male over there talking to Gary and Alicia?" Tanya motioned with an extravagant wave of chrome-tipped nails.

"I see him," Lacey agreed, thinking privately that

Mona's gown was clashing terribly with the wide, ornamental pants she had chosen to wear that evening. The full-cut pants were done in a metallic-striped purple and the silk taffeta blouse was burnished gold. Lacey had chosen an embroidered purple velvet jacket to go with it. Delicate sandals completed the rich look.

"He's next on my list. Isn't he gorgeous?" Mona asked rhetorically.

"Very. Rich?"

"Naturally. I wouldn't have him on my list if he weren't." Mona looked mildly astonished at her neighbor's slow-wittedness. "You seem rather quiet tonight, dear. You really must get out and circulate a bit more. Shall I send that lovely man over to you? I can spare him for the evening."

"That's awfully generous of you, Mona—"

"Nonsense! What are friends for." Mona patted Lacey's arm affectionately. "I'll send him right over!"

Lacey opened her mouth to say it wasn't necessary but gave up as Mona swept off. Her neighbor was feeling generous tonight, and there was no stopping her when she had made up her mind anyway.

Lacey was watching Mona bear down on the unsuspecting male when a faint prickle of awareness made her glance toward the open front door. She caught her breath at the sight of Jed's familiar—and totally unexpected—figure.

For just an instant all of her initial reactions to him floated across her mind. A panther—lithe and slightly menacing. A sorcerer who confounded attempts to categorize and stereotype him. Her lover. The man she hadn't seen in three weeks.

179

He didn't see her at first and Lacey stood very still, watching as he scanned the crowd. He had continued to shave, she thought irrelevantly, and he was dressed in one of the outfits he had selected that day in Beverly Hills. The gold-streaked hair was combed casually back in what had become all the rage down at the salon where the "style" had been accidentally created. The polished boots beneath the dark, lean slacks complemented the suede jacket and the open-throated shirt. He looked terrific, she thought happily. Irresistible, in fact. But then he had been that from the first. Her designer's eye had seen the potential from the beginning, she decided with satisfaction.

Lacey was still in the process of congratulating herself when his head turned toward her and across the room their eyes met and locked. Lacey's heart skipped a beat as she saw the direct, flaring hunger in his gold and brown eyes. And then he started toward her with those long, gliding strides that reminded her so much of a large cat.

Belatedly Lacey found herself wondering what in the world he was doing here tonight. He was supposed to be in Santa Cruz! Her initial shock at seeing him wore off, and she remembered the Margarita in her hand. Hastily she took one last sip and put down the glass. Why wasn't he smiling? Why was he here in the first place? And why did he look a little as he had the night he'd found her trying to flee in the garden?

Her impulse to smile and hurry toward him died as she realized the extent of the hardness radiating from him. Jed Merlin was not in a pleasant mood. Disturbed sorcerers were dangerous, she thought vaguely. But why was he disturbed? She stood very still and waited.

"Hello, Lacey," he said very quietly, the deep voice

clearly audible above the surrounding din. "You look very
. . . L.A. tonight." He scanned her figure once, dismissing-
ly, and then once again met her eyes.

Lacey, who had been about to throw herself into his
arms, hesitated uncertainly. For the life of her she couldn't
understand the conflicting signals she was getting from
him. What was wrong?

"Hello, Jed. What . . . what brought you up from Santa
Cruz?"

This was ridiculous, she thought wildly. They should be
greeting each other with the ecstasy of lovers who had
been temporarily separated, not this strange wariness!

"That's obvious, isn't it?" He glanced around the colorful room. "I came for you. When you didn't return to
Santa Cruz, I realized there was no point waiting any
longer."

"But, Jed! You don't understand!" But Lacey was beginning to understand. He'd thought she wasn't coming
back to him. Explaining things to Jed Merlin when he was
in this mood could take some doing, she recalled with
vivid awareness. It hadn't been that long ago that she had
stood blinded in the garden and said almost those exact
words!

"What don't I understand, Lacey? That you got back
to Los Angeles and decided you couldn't give up the tinsel
after all?"

"Be careful, Jed, you're on the verge of making a fool
of yourself!" Lacey snapped, growing suddenly annoyed at
his lack of faith.

"I know," he shot back, his voice hardening abruptly.
"Watch this: I've come to tell you that you're going to
marry me, Lacey Holbrook!"

181

The startled silence in the room was deafening. With the southern California instinct for an interesting experience, everyone turned as if at a given signal and stared at the couple in the corner.

"Marry you!" Lacey stared at him as he stood eye-to-eye with her, only a foot away. *"Marry you!"*

"You heard me! If you won't come to me, I'll come to you, but it's damn well going to be on my terms. You're going to forget all that garbage about not needing a piece of paper to make it right."

"You agreed with me! You were the one who said it first in fact!" But her heart was singing and Lacey looked at him with a dawning joy.

"So I've changed my mind! What the hell are you going to do about it?" he challenged.

It wasn't Lacey whose voice was heard next, however, it was a frantic Mona Hawkins.

"Oh, my God! Isn't he magnificent? Somebody get me a pencil and some paper. Where on earth is my tape recorder? I've got to get this down. He's a natural! The only thing I'll change about him is his height! A couple of inches taller . . . No, no, I can just make the heroine shorter! For heaven's sake, where is my notebook!"

Out of the corner of her eye, Lacey saw Mona racing around like mad, scrabbling for her tape recorder. "Jed, Jed, of course, I'll marry you! I love you, damn it! I want to marry you more than anything else in the world. But will you please get me out of here? This is getting more than a little awkward! If you have any feeling for me at all, you will take me away from all this! Now!"

She watched the slow, dashing grin spread across his face as he stepped forward and scooped her up into his arms. Turning on one heel, he started for the door. The interested crowd parted readily, making way for him.

"I never could resist you when you turn masterful," he growled on the edge of laughter.

"Wait, wait. I've found the tape recorder." Mona hurried after the pair, waving the small machine. As she saw they were about to escape, she turned anxiously to one of the guests. "What color would you say his hair is? A sort of sun-shot lion's mane? Sand and gold? Damn! Why did he have to carry her off so quickly? He was absolutely perfect! So masterful, so raffish, so deliciously *male*!"

On that comment, Jed managed to hook his toe around the door and yank it shut behind him. Out in the hallway he carried Lacey the few steps to her own apartment and stood waiting impatiently with her in his arms as she dug out the key.

"Hurry up," he advised as she fumbled. "Us masterful, raffish types don't like to be kept waiting."

"No, no, *I'm* the masterful one, remember? You're the one who can't resist the forceful type." Lacey turned the key in the lock and pushed on the door.

A moment later Jed was kicking it shut behind him. He carried her over to the black leather sofa and sat down with Lacey in his arms. "Lacey, Lacey, do you mean it? You'll marry me without an argument? I don't have to threaten or coerce or otherwise exert myself unduly?" He looked dazed but enormously pleased with himself.

"Oh, Jed," she breathed, her arms entwined around his neck. "How could I resist you? You're perfect! Marrying you will make me the happiest woman on earth!"

He shut his eyes briefly in silent relief. She could feel the tension easing out of him. "Thank you, Lacey. I was afraid you would be dead set against the idea . . ."

"And I was afraid you would be dead set against it!"

"When you didn't come back to Santa Cruz, I couldn't wait any longer," he whispered throatily. "For three weeks I've been waiting. Every time I called you on the phone you sounded more and more hurried. I began to panic. I thought surely you were changing your mind about loving me. I was afraid I'd made a terrible mistake allowing you to come back here."

She silenced him with her fingers on his lips and smiled gently. "What do you think that party at Mona's was all about tonight?"

"I don't care what it was all about! You're here in my arms and you're going to marry me!"

"Jed, that was a farewell party for me! I've sold the interior design business. I was going to surprise you by showing up in Santa Cruz in a couple of days and moving in with you, lock, stock, and barrel."

"What? Oh, Lord! Are you telling me the truth, Lacey? You've sold out? You were going to leave L.A. for me? For good?"

"What's wrong? Don't you want me, darling?"

He stared at her as if he didn't know what to say. And then he began to laugh. He leaned back against the cushions and laughed until Lacey couldn't stand it anymore. Once more she silenced him, this time with the flat of her palm.

"What's so funny, damn it?" she demanded aggressively. "This was a big decision on my part, in case you don't realize it. There isn't another man on the face of the earth for whom I'd give up everything like this! You've got a hell of a nerve laughing at me!"

He looked at her over the edge of her hand, tawny eyes brimming with the humor in him. "Oh, Lacey, you don't know how much it means to me to hear you say you've walked away from everything for me. But that's not what I'm laughing at."

"What, then?"

"Don't glare at me, darling, things are going to be difficult enough to explain as it is!"

"I'm waiting," she said, tapping the couch with mock impatience.

"Honey, I'm here tonight because I just sold the company to Kali and the rest of the staff! I figured if you couldn't bring yourself to leave L.A., I would have to come and live here with you. I sure as hell didn't intend to go on as we have the past three weeks communicating by telephone!"

"You sold your firm? Jed!" She was overwhelmed with the news. Never in a thousand years would she have expected him to change his whole life for her.

He grinned ruefully, bending over to kiss the tip of her nose. "I suppose the reason you sounded so hurried on the phone during the past couple of weeks was because you were busy closing the business arrangements here? Why didn't you tell me, Lacey?"

"I wanted to surprise you! Oh, my God! I can't believe this! We'll starve!" But as the shock wore off, the laughter began to bubble up inside her.

"Not quite. I've got a five-pound tub of tofu down in the car. A farewell present from the new owners of the factory," he told her cheerfully. "Never let it be said I couldn't take care of my new bride!"

185

"This is crazy, Jed," she breathed. But Lacey had never felt happier in her life.

"I think it's kind of exciting. I like the idea of starting over from scratch with you. A long time ago you offered me a business proposition, Lacey Holbrook. I was a fool to turn it down the first time. But I've grown much smarter over the years. If the offer is still open, I'm taking you up on it."

Lacey's hazel gaze shone with the glow of her love. "You'll marry me and unite our empires?"

"I'll marry you and we'll build an empire together," he clarified. "Still sound interesting? A couple of born entrepreneurs like us should be able to take some unsuspecting place by storm."

She considered that. "You realize, of course, that Mona's heroes generally turn out to be disinherited dukes who regain their inheritance at the end of the story?"

"So I'm not quite perfect." He shrugged. "I'll bet I'm terrific at ripping off your bodice. In any event, you're my inheritance!"

"And that's another thing. Her heroines are usually tiny and petite and, oh, so beautiful." Lacey looked up at him wistfully.

"I much prefer the strong, non-fragile, oh-so-beautiful type myself," he assured her lovingly.

She smiled very brilliantly. "Do you really think I'm beautiful?" she asked, knowing full well she wasn't but quite prepared to hear him lie about the issue.

"You're perfect," he murmured, beginning to nuzzle interestedly at the curve of her neck. "Absolutely perfect. Oh, Lacey, I love you so much!"

"In that case, Jed Merlin," she whispered invitingly, "I

186

would like to take this occasion to tell you that the offer I made when I was thirteen years old is, indeed, still open. I propose that we get married and unite the family empires. Or lack thereof."

"Thank you, I accept."

He leaned farther back into the cushions, pulling her close. The nuzzling at her nape grew more serious and Lacey shivered blissfully as he grazed her ear very gently. She sighed and turned her head slightly to kiss his throat, inhaling the magical scent of him.

"Love me, Jed. I love you so much!"

His hands moved on her with the now-familiar magic and her clothing seem to fall aside. With trembling fingers Lacey returned the favor, tugging at his shirt, fumbling with the fastening of his slacks. All the while Jed told her of his love in that purring growl that ruffled her nerves and called to her senses.

Naked at last, Lacey felt herself lifted high in his arms once more as he surged up off the sofa and started toward the bedroom with her. She looked up at him, her nails playing with the hair on the back of his neck.

"You're getting awfully good at the masterful bit," she drawled. "Not planning on changing roles with me, are you?"

"There always was a little confusion on this point, wasn't there?" he observed, settling her lightly on the bed and coming down beside her. "But I suppose it doesn't matter in the long run. Neither of us can resist the other . . ."

"No," she agreed on a passionate sigh as his strong, sensitive hands coursed down the length of her body and found the curve of her hip. Her head tipped back on his arm and she reached up to draw his mouth down to hers. "But in your case the weapons are a little unfair. What chance does a woman like me have against sorcery? All the L.A. flash in the world can't fight it."

"I am what you've made me," he chuckled with blatantly false modesty.

"Unemployed?"

"The man of your dreams," he corrected smoothly.

"Oh, that. I told you that when I was thirteen." Lacey put out the tip of her tongue and touched his lip provocatively. Her arms wound around his neck and her body arched languidly beneath his hand.

"You always were a bossy, know-it-all little kid," he groaned. The tawny eyes were going gold with his rising passion.

"And now I'm a bossy, know-it-all, not-so-little woman," she finished contentedly.

"Who is as unemployed as I am. At least we're starting out on the same footing. But I've got some plans on how to occupy our time while we're waiting to build our new united empire."

He moved, closing the small distance between their bodies on a wave of passion and love that would last a lifetime.

## LOOK FOR NEXT MONTH'S
## CANDLELIGHT ECSTASY ROMANCES™